MURPHY KNEW HE WAS RUNNING OUT OF TIME . . .

There were three of them, he was certain of it now. The two shooters kept him pinned, and he guessed the third one was working off to the side to get a clear shot at him. He looked around the basin again, trying to find cover, and there was nothing. Nothing.

Except his dead horse. Forty feet to the horse, then another fifty feet to the rocks at the side of the basin opposite the attackers. It might as well be fifty miles. If he could draw the ambushers out a bit, get them to shoot fast and have to reload. Maybe. Maybe.

He fired six shots in the direction of the mountain and was up and running. Dirt spurted up all around him as he ran, and he felt the spot on his back where he was certain the bullets would pound into him . . .

He was going to make it through the snapping storm of lead, he was almost there . . . then the slug took him, drove him down . . .

———————————

"Satisfying. . . . Murphy is a tough, lonely romantic, and Cincherville's single unpaved street is as mean as they come."

—ALA *Booklist*

MURPHY's GOLD

Gary Paulsen

POCKET BOOKS

New York   London   Toronto   Sydney   Tokyo

POCKET BOOKS, a division of Simon & Schuster Inc.
1230 Avenue of the Americas, New York, NY 10020

Published by arrangement with Walker and Company

ISBN: 0-671-66944-3

First Pocket Books printing September 1989

10 9 8 7 6 5 4 3 2 1

POCKET and colophon are trademarks of
Simon & Schuster Inc.

Printed in the U.S.A.

CHAPTER 1

MURPHY SAT IN his office and stared at the dust motes riding the morning sun coming in the windows and tried not to think. Everything was upside down—nothing had changed and yet everything had changed.

He was still Al Murphy, working for Murphy's gold as the sheriff of Cincherville, Colorado—$64 a month and some beans and a room in back of the hotel. He was still tall, big-boned, curve-shouldered—with the quiet strength that came from the care and settled caution that were the result of walking into too many bar fights or tight corners where a word could turn into a knife or bullet.

Scars. He still had the same scars, except for a couple of new ones inflicted by Hardesty, the sinister banker who had killed several people, including little Sarah Penches. Not all the new scars were on

Murphy's body; the whole ordeal had left its mark on his mind, his soul. Now and then he would come awake at night, alone in the damp wet nest of his hotel bed, wishing there was a hell just so Hardesty could rot there. The intensity of his hatred frightened Murphy. That he could think such things upset him and whenever he awakened with those thoughts he fought them. Hardesty had been bad enough and deserved to be killed; now Murphy wanted only to be free of the memory, but he could not run from it or hide from it.

He moved his shoulder. There was still some ache from the long-ago bullet that had cut high on his arm in the fight with the two men in the saloon, a small ache that was leaving but came now and then in the mornings. He recalled the fight suddenly, felt it slide like a warm knife into his thoughts—the men with the guns, the melding with the recurring dream he had, about the smiling man who wanted to kill him. The fight had happened before Hardesty.

When there still had been the two men, he thought morosely—before he had killed them. When there had been a Hardesty. Before Murphy had killed him. In the town of Cincherville—before Murphy damnnear had killed the town.

Ah, well, there it was—the town. Murphy was doing nothing that he wanted to do, was being nothing that he wanted to be. Instead, he was living a way he had sworn he would never live again.

During his shoot-out with Hardesty, the fire from the oil in the harness shop had gotten out of control and before the townspeople could stop it—or contain it so that it could burn itself out—more than half the town was gone, turned to ashes and dirty smoke.

Cincherville was effectively dead. The store, the blacksmith shop, the café, the bank, and harness shop—all gone. Even the boardwalks on the mountain side of town were gone. Gone to ashes, he remembered, like the old song said—gone to ashes and dirt.

And with it, he thought then, with the smoke went any reason for him to stay. He had Midge, with her brown eyes and straight-up-and-down look, and what they had between them, the gentleness. He had that, and he was going to take her and leave Cincherville and the merchants' association and the stink from Hardesty and the stink from the smoke and the stink of death. Leave with Midge and find a place where the grass was always green, if he had to go all the way back to Iowa.

He stood suddenly, breaking the thought pattern before it became too depressing. Dreams—all kids' dreams. Might as well order a life out of the Monkey Wards catalog. Just to hell with what was real, and order what you want. I'll take an order of happiness and kids' dreams, a place with a small picket fence and some green grass and a woman waiting for me—just send that on by railway express, will you? Throw in some rosy skies and a sweet well and the smell of baking bread, maybe some clean sheets that I don't sweat in every night. . . .

"Damn." He said it evenly, almost gently. Not swearing so much as sighing.

All dreams, all from some kids' idea of what life should be. Beneath the dreams was the hard truth, that he and Midge had nothing. Everything Midge had saved—and God knows it was little enough,

7

cooking for the town and the miners who came in on business now and then from the busted-out mines in the hills above town—everything she had saved had gone up with the bank. Gone. As well as her café.

She had only the clothes on her back, and Murphy had little more. Before the Hardesty conflagration, he had saved nothing from his $64-a-month pay. He had his gun and an extra pair of pants and shirt to wear while the Wangsu family was washing the others. And so his and Midge's pretty talk of what they would do when this was over and that was over, all of the dream words, were gone up in smoke, just as the town had practically gone up in smoke.

He had turned in his badge but they could not afford to leave. They could do nothing because they had nothing. For a time, Murphy had considered just putting her on a horse and leaving, walking in front of the horse and leading her away with nothing, following the wind the way he had done when he was young, when he left the army and drifted into Cincherville. But he could not do that to Midge. Young, it would have been hard enough, but they were in their mid-thirties, and to start new with nothing, to follow the wind, would be too hard for them. Milt Hodges had recovered from where the slug from Hardesty's bull gun had taken him. Hodges had lived at Doc's until he was well, then had moved on. But he was young and single and had only himself to think on.

So Murphy and Midge had stayed. There was never an agreement, never a word said of it, of what they would do, could do. He had looked at her and she had looked at him and they had known that they could not leave. At first Midge had moved into his room in the hotel and he had slept in the jail, mostly for appearances' sake. Neither of them cared what people said—not that anybody, for any reason, would dare say anything bad of or about Midge where Murphy could hear it—and they had shared what they were more than once. But Midge felt comfortable with them not openly living together and Murphy had agreed.

To his complete amazement, the town had rebuilt. He would have thought—*did* think—that Cincherville would die a little more each day until it completely disappeared, as so many of the other mining towns had done. But he had been wrong.

There had not been an explosion of civic pride or effort—Murphy was right about that much. The merchants of Cincherville were not particularly inspired or driven by anything, except need and greed. Cincherville had rebuilt more in a series of responses to need, the way a cold snake will crawl sluggishly from the shade into the sun to get warm, more as a reflex action, than in response to inspiration or pride.

While the buildings were gone, there were still people, and they had needs. Somebody needed food, somebody else needed hardware, and so a new dry-goods store was built of old wood from the nearby mines that had gone under.

Some miners came into town and needed harnesses for the mules they drove into the ground, literally, in the mines; the miners did not care what had happened in town, they just wanted harnesses. So a harness shop was put up with more old lumber.

Then, because miners were coming into town and

wanted to eat, Midge hired Old Man Sorenson for thirty dollars to come and put up a small frame building that she named, simply, Midge's Place—and she was back in business, cooking on an old range she found in back of the hotel in a pile.

And because the miners wanted to drink and raise hell, somebody showed up with two barrels and a plank and a crib girl and there was a saloon. That brought a gambler or two and another crib girl and because there were miners raising hell and crib girls and cheap whiskey, there was trouble. So they came to Murphy—the merchants from the old association—with the smile and oil of somebody wanting something for nothing. They came to Murphy and asked him to keep the peace and order.

Peace and order.

At one time he had worked for that. He had used that as justification for what he did, the way he acted, the way he ran the street and the town. *For the peace and good order of the people.*

That was before Hardesty. Now the townspeople had come like small dogs smelling around, asking him to ensure peace and order—except they wanted to pay him less, wanted him to do it for only forty a month and found. Less than a top hand on a run-down ranch would get. They wanted peace and good order for a bargain price.

He had not even spoken when they said that. Instead he had just looked at them, the four merchants who still remained in Cincherville. They stood in his office in a small circle: Johnson, with his weak smile; Emerson, with his store-white soft hands;

Backus, with his back-shot hair trying to cover the bald spot; and Danielson, who could not look Murphy straight in the eyes because Murphy once had pulled him off a crib girl, where he had passed out, and then had sent him, stinking of sweat and puke and cheap whiskey, home to his wife.

They wanted a bargain and he had just stared at them until Emerson finally coughed and shrugged. "Of course," the merchant had said, "it was just an idea—you know, until we can get back on our feet. But I guess it wasn't such a good idea at that, was it?"

And Murphy had stared, quietly, waiting, until they told him they would give him the same $64 a month and he had nodded them out. One short nod to make them leave the office.

So nothing had changed, and yet everything was different.

Murphy looked out his window on the street, turning slightly to do so, and as his nose came over his shoulder he noticed something. This morning he had gone to Midge's for some eggs and fried potatoes and pepper, and in the back, not a room but just behind a partition, he had held her for a moment and she had left some powder or scent that smelled of lavender on his shoulder. The smell came up from his shoulder now and made him think suddenly of Midge. . . .

It would take him a year. In a year, if he saved all that he could, he might have enough so they could leave. Keep a year smooth and don't make trouble or get shot—just keep a year even and he would have a few dollars and they could leave. He owed this town nothing. Owed them no loyalty now, nothing. He would skate for a year, stay out of trouble, and get some money and leave.

That was the plan.

Spend the year bringing old drunk Clyde in to puke it out every night, watching his back to stay safe, and to hell with the town.

To hell with them.

He opened the door and stepped out into the midday sun. Instinctively, he moved to the side of the door, as was his habit. A precaution, one of several tricks meant to make him less of an open target. He had taken a step when a small figure came from the side of the frame-clapboard building that was the sheriff's office and jail.

It was Wong Ny, the small girl who was the daughter of Wangsu and his wife, Tonsun—the Chinese couple who lived north of town in a series of huts and did laundry, cooked, grew a garden to supply vegetables for the café and store, raised chickens to sell for meat and eggs, kept goats for milk and cheese, did sewing and mending and some baking (small cakes that Wong Ny sold on the street and that melted in the mouth).

They generally kept to themselves and there had not been once that Murphy's services had been needed, other than when some drunken miners—some years ago—had tried to go out and raise hell and ". . . cut the pigtails off the Chinese boys." By the time Murphy had arrived, Wangsu—using a kind of polished hardwood staff—had three of the miners down in the dirt, while the fourth and last one was holding his jewels and sounding like he was asking for his mother, leaving Murphy nothing to do but carry the garbage back into town.

Murphy looked down at Wong Ny and smiled. He could not guess her age. Perhaps seven, although she was so petite that she might have been five. Her hair was cut straight across in even bangs, then dropped on each side of her face, falling down to make another even cut all around the back. She wore a spotless pair of straight cotton pants and a tunic with a high collar, all in deep blue, and she looked up at him very seriously.

"Can I help you?" Murphy squatted in front of her. "Is there something I can do?"

She still said nothing, but nodded with great solemnity and handed him a piece of paper. It was brown, had been cut evenly from a wide-lined, coarse paper note pad, and on it, printed in penciled block letters, was a message:

PLEASE THANK TO COME TO US. WE MAY HAVE NEED OF YOU.

Murphy studied the note for a moment, then looked to Wong Ny again. "Is this from your father?"

She slowly shook her head.

"From your mother?"

This time she nodded, then reached out a small hand and pulled at his sleeve, pointing at the same time to the north end of town.

"Is something wrong?" he asked.

But now she didn't answer, didn't even nod, only pulled at his sleeve so that he stood and followed her.

He straightened his hat to settle the sweatband in the right place and took short steps to hold his stride down to hers. As he walked, he wondered why, now—after four months of sitting in boredom—for the first time the hairs on the back of his neck were tightening.

CHAPTER 2

THE SMALL LINKED huts that comprised the Wangsu home were probably not over half a mile from the middle of Cincherville. But at the north end of town, the road took a tight series of curves around a stand of large boulders and tailing piles that were left from some exploration holes dug back when there was thought of heavy strikes in the area. They all had proved worthless, or nearly so. Now and then there would be color hit, but it was rare, and in the end there was mostly just holes and piles.

The huge mounds served, however, to set the Wangsus apart so that some people in Cincherville referred to the dwellings as Chinatown or Little China, which Murphy knew was ridiculous. But the setting apart added to the mystery of the Chinese, and in the main kept people away, except for a few incidents of racial unrest, such as had brought Mur-

phy once before. Although there were Chinese working all over the West, on the railroads and in the
mines—indeed, in San Francisco they talked of a
proper Chinatown, run by tong lords with their own
government and vicious law—they were not really
accepted or understood by the majority of people in
the towns.

Murphy had heard the gossip, the hissed comments.
He had heard whiskey-talk in the saloon or in the
street about their women, trash-talk; or about how
they believed in devils and opium smoke gods, had
recipes for eating white people; how they were completely controlled by one old man back in China who
was their god and who could order them to do
anything, even kill themselves, and they would do it.
Some people said the Chinese did not care as much as
other people about living; or how they could not see
colors or count higher than twenty; or, finally, that
they were not truly human. All garbage talk. Talk from
the same people who believed in night witches or
black cats, people who found their god in a whiskey
bottle.

Murphy knew the Chinese as tough, intelligent
workers—respected them for it—with strong families; people who never caused trouble (another plus to
somebody who spent a large portion of his life cleaning it up) and who seemed always to give a fair share
for what they got. Most of this he had gleaned from
the one brush with Wangsu when Murphy had arrived
too late to help. Even though that was his sum total
knowledge of the Chinese people, he believed more in
what he saw than what he heard, and what he saw in
the Wangsu family, in the limited time he had seen or

known them, filled him more with awe than anything else. They could come into an area like the north of Cincherville, where the dirt was said to be worthless, and pull rich gardens out of soil; they could take a little dirt and some water and herbs and make a blue dye so rich that the tunic on Wong Ny seemed to catch and hold the sun as she walked with Murphy. They could make something from nothing, whereas Murphy had spent a lot of time working with street people who seemed to be dedicated to just the opposite—turning something into nothing.

He and the girl came around the final bend in the road and Wong Ny stopped for a moment.

Before them lay the Wangsu home. Really a string of frame huts, they somehow had an Oriental feeling to them—perhaps because when Wangsu made them, all of lumber from abandoned mines, he had let the roof eaves overhang three or four feet, more than was usual. From each of the eaves there hung a clay pot in the shape of a mythical animal head—dragons and lions, ornately beautiful, made from earthen clay found in the tailings. In each pot there was a plant, and the plants had leaves that hung down, lush and green, to cover the walls of the shelters in strings of vines. It made the dwellings look exotic, beautiful, and completely out of place in the high desert and rocks that surrounded Cincherville.

Off to the side, to the right as Murphy viewed it standing with Wong Ny, there was a neatly rowed, intensely green garden—well over an acre. And to the side of that were a chicken pen enclosed with wire and a carefully laid-out goat pen. As Murphy and the child stopped, hesitated, the screen door to the center dwelling opened and Tonsun came out. She was a larger version of Wong Ny, even to the blue pants and tunic—though she was still small next to Murphy. Just outside the door she stopped, acknowledged Murphy, and waved him to come to the house. She then turned and said several fast words in Chinese—Murphy always thought it sounded like water running over small pebbles, falling and falling but never stopping—then she called to Murphy.

"Come now. Come now. We have tea. We sit and we have tea."

Inside the door he stopped. Wong Ny took him by the hand and led him into the center house, following her mother. Wong Ny stepped to the side and gestured him forward. The room was nearly empty. In the center was a low hardwood table, perhaps a foot and a half high, polished to a sheen, and the shelves on the side of the room were neatly packed with small boxes and pots. In the center of the table was a cane mat and on the mat sat a clay pot emitting steam. Two small cups—they looked like oversized thimbles to Murphy—were next to the pot.

Tonsun stood on the other side of the table and gestured for him to sit. The room, the table, the cups, even Tonsun and her daughter—everything—were so small that Murphy felt like a hulking giant.

He kneeled stiffly at the table and admired Tonsun as she gracefully lowered herself on the other side, settling like a leaf falling from a tree. She poured an amber, spicy-smelling tea into the two cups—still without saying a word—and signed for Murphy to drink. He picked up the cup, his large hands folding around the tiny vessel. He sipped the tea, hot and invigorating.

When he had come before, the one time when Wangsu had handled the miners, he had come in for tea but it had been in larger cups and tasted more like regular tea. What he was drinking now was not just a flavor, it was an ambrosia that went into his nasal passages, into his mind. It was a very special tea, and this whole thing—his being summoned here mysteriously by Wangsu's favorite daughter, the setting, the room, Tonsun—all of it piqued his curiosity. Once he started to say something, to ask, but he held his tongue and waited. There was something she wanted, something new and different.

He waited.

Once a poet-minister had come through Cincherville. Must have been seven, eight years earlier—well before the small boom hit that made the town at least partially grow, before they found the small color. Murphy thought of him now as he sipped the tea. The minister had been a strange duck, kind of a cross between someone wanting to spread the Gospel and and an orator standing on a stage and spouting poetry. For two or three months he had stayed in town, getting a bite of food here and there, stopping to preach or emote and recite poetry any time he could get two people to stop long enough to listen.

Most people got sick of him in a week or two, but since he didn't do anything wrong and Murphy sort of liked him, Murphy didn't want to run him out of town, as he would other vagrants. The minister was a small thorn in the paw of the merchants' association

—they didn't like anybody getting attention except them, didn't want the mind to stray from buying, one way or the other. Besides, even Murphy had to admit the fellow usually didn't make enough sense to clean a stable. Whether he talked Gospel or did poetry, it was all pretty much gobbledygook. But once he had said something about China that stuck with Murphy, about being civilized:

> "In far off Chinaland,
> they drank tea with a pinkied hand,
> two thousand years before Christ."

Murphy thought of that now, watching Tonsun drink. She didn't seem to hold the cup. Rather, it floated up, pulling her small hand with it, and she sipped the tea so delicately it made him feel more than awkward, as if he could break something by just being there.

He studied her eyes when she was looking down briefly to pour more tea. They were brown and even, almond shaped. She had the same beauty as Midge—sensible beauty. Beauty you came home to. But there was something else there as well, a tightness that came from, what, worry? He couldn't be sure, but he had seen it before in other people. Sometimes he felt that was about all he had seen—that tightness. He eased up on his knees a bit to take the weight off his toes, which were jamming into his boots and pinching off circulation.

When he moved, his gunbelt creaked, and the sudden sound broke the silence, broke the spell.

Tonsun put her cup down. "All the same—white people, China people. All the same?"

For a moment he said nothing, then realized she was asking a question, soliciting his opinion. He thought a moment of all the stories and garbage, then nodded slowly and said, "All the same. All people." True enough, he thought—everybody got that pinched look in the corners of the eyes when they needed Murphy's help. It had been there with the Penches when they found out about little Sarah . . . he pushed the thoughts away. *All the same.* He wondered where it was going. She didn't bring him out here just to talk about all people being alike.

"All the same," she continued, "white people, China people, put money in town. Put money in town each year to pay for town. All the same."

She was getting away from him now, and he signed her to stop. "What do you mean, put money in town? I don't understand."

She looked at him. "For town—spend money for town, all the same white store owners. Put money in town."

Taxes. Murphy nodded—they had been paying money into the town fund. Damn. He hadn't known the merchants' association was that low—to make a Chinese family pay taxes when it lived out of town. "I understand. All the same, you pay money for town like them. But you shouldn't have to."

She studied him as if he were mad. "All the time pay, all the month pay, all the years pay, China people always pay. Pay to work. Pay to live. Pay to be.. All the time China people pay."

21

He nodded, thinking on it, chewing on it. "It stinks."

Tonsun raised her eyebrows, her bangs arching. "Stinks?"

He decided against explaining and shook his head. "It's nothing. So white people and Chinese people pay, all the same, for the town. I understand that. But why do you say this?"

She frowned, thinking of a way to put things. "All the same white people and China people pay for the law?"

For the law? Now he frowned. "How do you mean —pay for the law?"

She settled back for a moment, sighed, then shrugged. "All the same China people pay like town people pay for law. Pay for law. Don't know other way to say."

He shook his head. "You don't pay for the law—the law just is. The law is for everybody."

She stopped him now with a raised hand, delicate fingers fluttering. "Law for China people all the same as for white people?"

Ahh, he thought—there it is. She doesn't mean the law. She means me. Will I work for her as I work for the town? Hell, he thought, probably better, the way I feel about the town. He nodded. "All the same. Same law for whites and Chinese people. Why do you ask this? Do you have a law problem?"

Now she hesitated longer, and he thought he saw moistness in the corner of her eye. Not yet a tear but moving that way. Her voice had a slightly brittle sound to it—on the edge of breaking. "Have a law problem—yes."

"Is there trouble?"

"Have trouble, yes. Have big trouble." She began to cry now, silently letting the tears flow, moving her shoulders with it. "Think have big, big trouble."

"What's the matter, Tonsun?"

"Wangsu gone."

Initially he had wondered why Wangsu wasn't here. The smiling, stocky man would not have missed a chance to say hello. Murphy had decided he was in town gathering laundry or selling vegetables. Come to think of it, Murphy had not seen Wangsu in some time. Days. Several days. Maybe a week. "Where is he?"

Tonsun shook her head in exasperation. "No. Don't know where gone. Just gone—gone from here."

"You mean he's missing?"

She nodded excitedly. "That way gone. Missing. All the same . . ."

"How long has he been gone?"

She thought. "Six day. No, seven day. All the same a week. He's been gone seven day."

Murphy had a sinking feeling. Seven hours was a cold trail. Seven days was a lifetime when somebody was missing. Wangsu could have been out hunting and fallen and broken a leg—anything. If anybody was lost for seven days without water, that was it. . . . "Are you sure he isn't on a trip, hasn't just gone without telling you?"

She shook her head emphatically. "No. No do— not even one night. Always say, always tell."

"Could he be visiting somebody?"

She didn't answer. There was no need, and he felt foolish for asking the question. There were no other

Chinese within a hundred miles, perhaps further. And they did not "visit" locally except to pick up laundry or sell in town.

"Why did he leave?" he asked.

She shrugged. "Don't know."

"No, I mean when he left—what was the purpose of his leaving? Was he going into town with laundry?"

Something there now, he thought. Something in the eyes, but she quickly shut it down. It was only there for a second, and Murphy thought he might have imagined it. Something hidden.

She shook her head then. "No. He was going with package, to mail package."

Murphy nodded. Wangsu came to town during the first week of every month, usually on Friday. He'd show up with his package for San Francisco before the stage came in, the one that tied in with the railway over in Two Buttes. Once Murphy had stopped him and asked him what was in the package he mailed each month. Wangsu had smiled quickly and said, "Presents for family."

"In San Francisco? You have family there?" Murphy had replied.

Wangsu had explained that he did not have family in San Francisco but did have a large family back in China. Every month he sent them a package with "presents," which Murphy guessed was a small amount of money. He sent the package to a Chinese broker in San Francisco, who in turn sent the package on to his family. Wangsu told him that many Chinese families in America did the same thing. Sent "presents" back to the old country through brokers in San Francisco, and Murphy got the impression from

Wangsu that it was a considerable business—the brokerage of family "presents" heading back to China.

He eased forward again, restoring circulation to his aching feet. "So he was going with the package, and he left the house and you haven't seen him again? Is that it?"

She nodded. "Is that way. He left and we haven't seen. All the same can find for China person as for white person?"

Murphy stood slowly, weaving a bit. His legs were cramped and both calves were asleep. "I'll try—all the same, yes. Can you remember if he said anything, did anything that might help me?"

She thought, shook her head. "No. Just go, Wangsu just go and not come back. . . ."

She was lying. He was certain of it. Not about Wangsu being gone, her grief was too genuine for that, but she was holding back, lying about something. Questions, he thought, all the questions waiting to be answered truthfully were somewhere in a cave in barrels, stored, never to be answered. One thing he had learned: Everybody always lied to the law. And Tonsun was doing it now.

Two questions puzzled Murphy. Wangsu disappeared not on the first Friday in the month, but near the end of the month. Why lie about him taking a package in to mail?

And the second question: Why wait a week to report a man missing? If he had never done anything like this, why wait a whole week? If the tears were real and she was as heartbroken as she seemed, why wait a week?

"Can find?" she asked when his hand was on the door. "Can find Wangsu?"

He turned to see her eyes full of hope, and he responded by smiling, but out of kindness rather than any flicker of hope. It was not part of his job to have hope.

Questions, he thought, questions and lies, all stored in barrels in a cave somewhere. Maybe when he died he would find the answers. "I'll try," he said to Wangsu's wife. "All the same, Tonsun, I'll try."

Outside the sun was hot, cooking down on him. Noon, time for lunch at Midge's, lunch and talk. He started walking back to town, thinking of the questions.

It was the questions that Tonsun could have answered but didn't, he thought, that were the most important. Questions.

CHAPTER 3

AFTER THE HARDESTY mess, after they had asked him to stay on and he had known that he and Midge could not leave, there came a time for Murphy when he did not want to do anything. He had sat in the office, looking out the window, brooding, sometimes not shaving for two, three days, just thinking and staring out at nothing. Doc Hensley had tried to pull him out of it, came over to the jail and brought a bottle.

"Got to get your brain going again," Doc had said. "Fire up the cells and get it going. . . ." But it had not worked. It wasn't so much that Murphy was down as that he felt he was wasting his time. Even with Midge, with all of it, he felt it was all just a waste of time, and he had tried not to do anything; he had tried not to do his job. He was there, drawing the pay, but some part of him said to hell with it and he tried to just spend the time.

He couldn't do it. Even with that feeling, sitting staring out the window at the street, he could feel what was happening, could smell what was going on. He could not stop thinking and doing law any more than a hound with an injured leg could keep from running deer. It was, in the end, part of what he was—and when he realized it and accepted it, he was surprised to feel relieved. He stood up one day and shaved and settled the gun in place and went back to work, letting the street come to him, smelling and feeling and knowing that he would do it even if he didn't want to. Somehow there was purpose in it—the automatic way he did the law. A way to live.

He found that it was possible to know things without knowing for sure how he knew them; found that some part of his mind or soul took in information and kept track of it until one day he would be thinking and suddenly the knowledge was there. It was as if he felt the pulse of the town all the time, without knowing he was doing it, just taking everything in while the outward part did the rest of the job.

Now as he sat at Midge's and waited for food, he let the knowledge come. He started with the questions. Why did she lie about Wangsu going to mail the package?

"Are you hungry today?" asked Midge, coming out of the kitchen. "Medium, heavy—how much?"

He smiled up at her from the corner table. It had become his table because it was the only table backed into a corner where he could see both the door and windows while he ate. He and Midge had never said anything about it being his table or the reason for his choosing that one, yet it was understood. Always the job was there—even in his choice of dining tables. Three other men, all miners and all strangers to Murphy, sat at a table by the windows, tucking in enormous amounts of meat and potatoes covered with brown biscuit gravy.

"Fairly hungry," Murphy said. Something about the tea he had sipped with Tonsun had made him hungry. Triggered his tongue and made him want to eat. Normally he ate a light noon meal and kept his belly empty in case he had to work. No, he thought, that's kidding myself. He ate a light meal because if he got gutshot he didn't want the food messing things up. Always that was there, too—the same awful dream. The bullet in the dream leaving the gun of the smiling man in the saloon and coming slowly across the room to hit his stomach just above the navel, making the little puff of dust when it hit.

Midge nodded and went back into the kitchen to return a moment later with a plate heaped with potatoes and pot roast. Gravy covered everything, and she had a plate of bread slices in the other hand.

"God." Murphy snorted. "I'll never get around that. . . ."

"Growing boys." She laughed. "Do what you can and I'll give the rest to the street dogs."

"Not likely."

He paid her a dollar—the full amount—and she took the money into the kitchen and put it in a jar. At first she had told him not to pay, but he had insisted. Since they both were saving all the money they could, she set aside whatever he paid her in the jar. It was another way to save, to leave. She came back out, found no new customers, and sat down with Murphy.

"I expected you for coffee this morning." She brushed hair out of her face. Sometimes she used her hand, at other times she pushed her lower lip out in a pout and puffed wind to blow the hair back. He found both ways fetching and could not see her do it without feeling warmed by it. Something about the gesture made him want to reach over and push the hair away. Just as he sometimes wanted to wipe the perpetual flour smudge off her chin.

"Had some business out at Wangsu's place." He ate a piece of meat, chewing carefully, slowly. Then, between bites, he told her of talking to Tonsun, leaving nothing out, including the fact that Wangsu's wife had lied. When he had finished telling Midge, he was also done eating, had eaten it all (hoping woefully he would not get gutshot this afternoon) and felt as full as a tick. He sipped coffee that Midge brought. Two men came in and joined the three miners. Midge waited on the new customers—one of them a miner Murphy recognized from the McCormick hole west of town. The other was another new man, which made four new men in town in one day—and that was unusual.

Midge sat again and he noticed that she sat much as Tonsun had settled in back of the table—gracefully lowering onto the chair. Like a falling leaf. *All the same,* he thought, smiling inwardly, white ladies and Chinese ladies, all the same.

"Why do you think she lied?" Midge took a sip from his cup.

He shook his head. "I'm not sure. She probably doesn't want me to know where he was really going when he left. That's how that stacks. But I can't think why she waited a week to tell me he was gone. That doesn't run very well, except that my head keeps coming back to the package."

"The one he mailed each month?"

"Yeah. I don't know why but somehow I feel the package has something to do with all of this. . . ."

"I don't know if it helps, but Wangsu came to the back door one day on his way to mail the package. He was bringing me some beet greens, and he put the package down next to the pump in the kitchen. When he got ready to leave, I picked the package up to hand it to him and almost dropped it because it was so heavy."

"Heavy?"

Midge nodded. "A lot heavier than you'd expect from a small package. Perhaps five or more pounds, and it couldn't have been a foot long, maybe less, and six inches high and across."

Murphy filed that bit of information, was going to say more but an argument exploded at the table with the four new miners. Trouble often came this way, he thought. It came from nothing. Without thinking, he was on his feet and halfway to the table just in time to see a knife come out and make a flicking cut down the arm of one of the miners.

The man bellowed in pain and grabbed his arm, which was laid open from shoulder to elbow and seeping blood. He fell backward, tipping the table.

Murphy had his Smith .44 out now but had not

eared the hammer back. It was a double action so he could shoot fast if he needed to, but instead he pointed it at the man with the knife.

"Hold it," he said, sharply. "Now, the knife on the floor."

For a time, a part of a second, the man defied him. Murphy could see it in his eyes, had seen it many times. The white-hot flash of anger—anger that could kill—came up, and the man was going to come at him.

"Now," Murphy said again, not loudly, but as he would talk to a dog that was getting ready to bite him. "Now the knife goes down or you do. *Now.*"

Sense came into the man's eyes. It was like watching a dawn, Murphy thought, like watching the sun come up. The miner had been crazy with anger, and sense came back. Instead of dropping the knife, he kneeled slowly and set it carefully on the floor, then stood again.

"Everybody up against the wall."

The man on the floor held his arm and moaned, not moving, trying to stop the bleeding with his hand and not succeeding. The other three turned and faced the wall and Murphy searched them.

"I'm bleeding out, I'm bleeding out . . . ," the wounded man mumbled but Murphy didn't listen. It was a shallow cut, wasn't spurting the rich blood of an artery, and he would be fine. Some stitches, nothing more. Murphy knew blood. The puke blood from drunks, the pouring blood from head wounds when he hit somebody with a pistol barrel, the mouth blood from fights, the small blood from bullets where they went in and the big blood where they came out—he knew blood. ·

"Better get a towel," he said to Midge, "or rags or something before he messes the floor up."

Midge hurried to the kitchen and came back with some sacking she had made into a dish towel. She stopped and wrapped the man's arm with it, soaking up some of the blood. "Should I get Doc?" she asked Murphy.

He nodded and Midge rushed off for Doc Hensley. Then Murphy turned back to the three men leaning against the wall. "All right. Sort it out for me."

A look passed between them and they said nothing.

"I'll say it once more—sort it out for me." Murphy took a stance with his legs slightly apart, his weight balanced on the balls of his feet, the Smith held in his right hand, an extension of his arm. "Talk now."

"We just had an argument." It was the man on the floor, still holding his arm and moaning, who spoke through clenched teeth. "It just got out of hand."

Get them talking. A hundred, no a hundred thousand fights and he had settled them all by getting them talking. When somebody talked he didn't fight. It was the quiet ones who did you up for winter, the ones who didn't talk. "Who started it? What was it about? Talk."

More silence. Murphy nudged in the kidneys the man who had used the knife. Not a blow, not the kind that could put a man on his knees puking, but a reminder—a nudge with the barrel of the Smith. Then he said, "Start with your names and why haven't I seen you around here before?"

The names meant nothing to him. The one with the knife had an odd name—Clanson—but the rest were just Irish names. They said they were miners, but he already had guessed that. They wore coarse work shirts with longhandles, though it was summer and hotter than a stove top in the afternoon, and jeans with rivets in the pocket. Miners' jeans. Lots of dirt. Not just dirty, but dirt ground deep down and in, until you couldn't get it out with an ocean of soap and water, and a stink so high you could see it coming off them like summer waves.

Said they were new miners. They talked and he seemed to listen but something about what they were saying was all bull and he knew it, could tell by the way they looked at each other, the way their eyes tightened in the corners and the way they talked slow, thinking of each word. But they couldn't be lying about being miners, the stink gave them away; and they couldn't be lying about being new to town— Murphy had never seen them before. So what were they trying to hide?

"Enough," Murphy said and took a step back. "Walk out ahead of me, one at a time, easy and slow. . . ."

"What the hell . . . where are you taking us?" Clanson started to turn.

"To jail."

"Jail? On what charges?"

"I'll think something up. Walk."

"But, hell, man, we were just arguing. Pooter isn't going to press charges, are you, Pooter?" Clanson looked at the man on the floor, who shook his head emphatically.

"It just got out of hand—not a big thing," the wounded man replied.

Murphy said nothing, motioned to the door with his chin. "Walk."

Clanson held back. Craft came into his eyes. "So there's one of you and four of us—five with Pooter. . . ."

Murphy waited. "You're just about to make the biggest mistake of your life. Don't."

Clanson studied him, measured it, weighted it, and decided Murphy meant business. The muzzle of the Smith, steady and even and looking like a railroad tunnel, had a lot to do with his reconsideration.

Murphy saw the challenge go out of him, saw Clanson check it like a dog smelling a post and then leave it, walk away from it and start for the jail. As they got to the door Midge came in with Hensley, who was in his shirtsleeves with blood on his shirt, carrying his black bag.

"I left in the middle of lancing a boil. This better be necessary. . . ." He faded off as he saw the man on the floor, struggling to stand, holding his arm. "Ahh—I see." Doc looked at Murphy. "Can he come to the office?"

Murphy nodded. "I'll lock these four up and come over for him later." He turned to the man with the cut arm. "You try to take off and I'll cloud up and rain all over you, understand?" But it was a needless warning. Pooter, if that was really his name, was starting into light shock and wasn't about to run anywhere. His legs got rubbery and Doc had to help him through the door.

It took Murphy five minutes to get the other four

across the street and into a cell. His jail consisted of a frame building; the office area was in front of the cell portion, which was made of two-by-sixes overlapped and nailed flat to each other to make a solid six-inch wall. The cell section was separated by a frame wall and had a doorway, but no door. Clyde, one of the town drunks (sometimes on payday nights Murphy thought the whole town was made up of drunks), was sleeping and puking it off in one of the cells. The cell door wasn't locked and he started hacking and wheezing when he heard Murphy come in and lock up the four protesting miners.

"God, hold the noise down," Clyde muttered. "My head—ahh, God, my head." He went for the bucket in the corner of his cell, missed it, and sprayed the night's residue of cheap whiskey down his front and the wall. The smell immediately filled the cell area, overpowering even the stink of the miners, and Clanson swore.

"You aren't going to put us in with that. God, man—look at it." He pointed a thumb at Clyde, who stood in his filth with whiskey sores on his face and throat that made him look like a leper. "It's got some kind of disease. . . ."

Murphy had known Clyde before he started to drink, had watched him go from being a normal clerk who worked at the dry-goods store and lived in one of the other back hotel rooms to being something that crawled in the night and wet his pants. He had no disease other than cheap whiskey and bad luck and ruined life—it could be anybody. Murphy tried to be nice to Clyde, even when Clyde was mean and stupid on snakehead whiskey, because Murphy understood some of life and luck and how it could go sour on a man.

He locked the cell door on Clanson and the other three, hung the key back in the office, and said nothing. Questions, questions. It was the things they didn't say that counted. Why the look between them, why lie about the fight, and what they were doing?

It was what they didn't say that he wanted to know—just as it was what Tonsun didn't say that was important.

He stepped into the street, took fresh air into his lungs to knock out the jail stink, and started walking to Hensley's to get the other man.

Always questions.

CHAPTER 4

DEAD TRAILS—WANGSU was a dead trail.

With the five miners locked up, Murphy stalked through town. The saloon was still pretty much closed, although the two crib girls were hanging some laundry in back of the saloon on a rope between two poles. Too early for many customers. What were the girls' names, Murphy pondered—oh, yeah, Flora and Fawn. He smiled. Couple of farm girls from Iowa who had dreams about the West. Going to find husbands and live high. Probably on their way to San Francisco or Virginia City when they ran out of time and money and luck, all at once.

Murphy stopped by the clothesline—all underwear hanging in the still heat—and nodded to Flora. Or was it Fawn? No, he decided it was Flora. "Afternoon."

She pushed back a loose bit of hair, and he thought again about all women being the same—hers was the same gesture Midge or Tonsun would have used. Flora had heavy arms, a heavy body with large breasts, but not fat—healthy heavy. Stout. Miners liked them that way—healthy and stout.

"Some law problem?" Flora's eyes were suspicious. She and Fawn worked the edges and she knew it. They were not accepted, but were tolerated by the towns-people because the miners wanted them and whatever the miners wanted . . . but they worked the edges.

Murphy shook his head. "Maybe a little informa-tion. I'm trying to find Wangsu and I wondered if you'd seen him."

"The Chinaman who does all the selling and laun-dry?"

He nodded.

She thought, frowned and shook her head. "Not for a while . . . some days back we bought some vegeta-bles from him. We do our own laundry but we like to buy fresh vegetables. They're good for the health, you know. I heard that carrots can cure . . . well, you know."

"But you haven't seen him?" Murphy brought her back. "Recently?"

She shook her head. "Not in four, five days—maybe a week. Why, what's wrong?"

Murphy didn't answer, thanked her, and moved on up the street. Dead trails. Some people moved but the town was pretty slow, getting ready for the night. There were day people and night people and they did not mix. Day people worked the stores and the blacksmith shop and hotel and café; night people worked the saloon and had little or nothing to do with the others.

Murphy was the only one who worked in both groups. Sometimes he thought he was the only reason the two could be in the same place, because he was there to act as a buffer. He went to the dry-goods store—a new man named Ralph Weston owned it. All the shop owners seemed the same. Pale, with veins close to the skin and thin, quick smiles, depending on how much profit they were making.

Murphy stopped at the counter and took a piece of rock candy out of the candy jar, sucked on it, and waited until Weston had finished filling an order for Clarissa Penches. The Penches hadn't moved on after the Hardesty mess, and that had surprised Murphy. Charley still worked powder at the McCormick hole and got by. But neither he nor Clarissa ever looked at Murphy. There was too much pain—some connection between Murphy and what had happened to Sarah was there. Too many painful memories. Clarissa took her flour sack of staples and left, ignoring Murphy's nod to her.

"Good day, Sheriff." Weston turned to him. "Can I get you something?"

"Other than the candy, you mean?" Murphy smiled. "No—I need a little information. When's the last time you saw Wangsu?"

Not in a week, perhaps more, Weston answered. The same as the others. But a flicker now, in his eyes, a flicker of something deliberately concealed, as with Tonsun and the miners, and Murphy caught it. God, he thought, I'm getting skitchy—damn job. I'm seeing things in everybody. But hunches were much to Murphy, hunches and movements—little things had saved his life more than once, more than a dozen times. A tiny flicker in a man's eyes was sometimes all the warning you had, and if you didn't pull it all up and move in that half a second, you were dead.

So the tiny thing in Weston's eyes. Something between Weston and Wangsu? Wangsu sold vegetables to the store, but why hide that? Why did he seem to worry about Wangsu?

Murphy suddenly had this picture of the small Chinese man slipping through town and running everything, his hands in everybody's business—he was more than Murphy had thought. There was the thought of Wangsu, the little man who did laundry, sold vegetables, but more now, more—Murphy kept running into another side to him. Wangsu knew more of the town, more of what was happening than he had let on; knew everyone from crib girls to shop owners. Knew something about Weston that Weston felt he had to hide, had to lie about?

Another thing not answered. Murphy thought of pushing it, seeing if he could get Weston to explain, but decided against it. Better to wait, let things develop on their own.

He took another piece of candy and went outside. Down the dusty road, kicking the powder with each step, to the harness shop, the new one, where he asked Tilman Peterson about Wangsu. Tilman had hands stained permanently from the leather dye he used, smelled of old harness and horse sweat and oil, smelled of the grease in his apron. His dark hair was slicked back and sticky because he kept wiping it out of his eyes with a hand soaked in oil. When he died, Murphy thought, they wouldn't need to bury him— just hang Tilman in the back. He was already cured.

Tilman said Wangsu had come once for some leather strapping to make a small harness for a burro. Two, three weeks before. Said that was the last he had seen of him, thank you, and all he wanted to see of any heathen who didn't worship the Gospel, thank you. Wangsu had paid cash, silver cash, for the leather and some brass rivets, and gone on his way. Anything else?

At least with Tilman, Murphy had not seen anything hidden. Tilman's hate—or was it fear?—was so obvious there could have been nothing between him and Wangsu.

Next, the hotel. Benny Peters in the hotel, a new man who had come after the town was rebuilt, had seen Wangsu exactly eight days earlier. He knew because Wangsu came for the linen to wash it, and he came every eight days. He had been due yesterday and hadn't come, so where the hell was he? Benny ran on and on, but he always ran on and on, so Murphy found nothing there. That left only the homes up in back of Front Street and Murphy spent the better part of two hours talking to several miners' wives. Wangsu had come through eight or nine days earlier, selling vegetables and eggs. One of the wives had seen him heading west with a burro and pack early one morning but couldn't remember which morning.

Then gone.

A week ago, according to Tonsun, who was most

certainly lying, Wangsu had left the house to mail his package and apparently walked off the face of the earth.

Dead trail.

And that, Murphy thought, heading back for his office, seemed to be the end of it as far as the town was concerned. He could drop it now, go back to Tonsun and tell her it was a dead trail and there was no sense in looking further—or he could take it one more step and leave the town, start checking the mines in the surrounding country. Talk about a needle in a haystack, he thought, looking to the livery stable where his big gray was kept. After his double ride with Milt Hodges, carrying the unconscious young man to Doc's, his other horse had been blown and broken. He'd had to put it down. But the Old Colonel used to keep a big gray gelding, three years old and a little froggy but good. Of course, Old Colonel was gone, killed with a pitchfork by Hardesty, but Wayne Elspeth, who had worked at the livery from time to time, took over running the barn, and soon smelled and looked a lot like the Old Colonel had looked and smelled—of horse crap and saddle stink.

Murphy had worked a deal with Wayne for the gray, eighty dollars and pay on Sunday. So Murphy had the gray now, close to sixteen hands, a good horse but shy in bad light or dark. Murphy started for the livery to saddle him, was halfway across the street when he heard the voice.

"Sheriff."

It stopped him and he looked back at the walk in front of the hotel. A large man—he'd never seen him before—stepped off the boardwalk and walked toward him in the road. He was wearing a dark suit with a leather vest, and the suit had to work to cover the muscles. He was as tall as Murphy and probably ten pounds heavier, with no fat, no fat at all. On his head was a derby, flat and even, and his face was the same—flat and even. Brown hair and eyebrows, a large mustache, reddish complexion. At his waist he wore a gunbelt and it was oiled leather but with no cartridge loops. An old army gunbelt, Murphy guessed, and nodded to himself when he saw the U.S. buckle. The man carried a .45 Long Colt in the holster, not low but straight across.

The light was all wrong, came from in back of the stranger a bit and into Murphy's eyes. He turned his body slightly sideways, eased his hand down to his gun. Ready. Always ready.

The man stopped four paces away and stood for a beat, half a beat, without saying anything. Then, in an even voice, said: "Name's Young. Arvis Young. I hear you got some of my men in your jail. . . ."

Murphy said nothing, was thinking that he would hate to have to fight this man in a fair fight. He wasn't just big, but all cord- and whip-hard. Of course fights were never fair—they were just fights. He'd hate to cross horns with this man in any form.

"Five of my men," Young prompted. "Miners. Something they did in the café and you arrested them."

Murphy nodded now. "They raised some hell, tipped a table. I've got them in a cell. So?"

Another hesitation, half a beat, as if Young were

contemplating several different things he might do before he did any of them, the way a rattler might hesitate just before he struck—then Young's face broke into a smile that had about as much cheer in it, Murphy figured, as a mortician's.

"Hell, Sheriff, I need those men. You know how they are. Mining is a tough business and they're rough men. If they raise a little hell now and then, that's part of life in a mining town, isn't it?" He reached inside his coat—Murphy nearly drew when the hand moved —and pulled out a wallet. "If there is some fine or fee . . ."

My gold, Murphy thought—I could take bribes. I've never done it, but I could take bribes. In truth, the way fines were levied was basic. Drunk and disorderly was five dollars, damage was whatever it cost, plus twenty dollars. Murphy collected the fines—a circuit judge came up from Denver if needed but it was a rough trip, last eleven miles by coach, and they didn't like to do it—so Murphy turned fines over to the town council, really just the merchants' association. Murphy had never, not once, kept the money but it crossed his mind now. He shook his head. "It's not that easy. They did some damage at the café. That's got to be covered."

Young's smile remained fixed, even, but his eyes glittered with anger. Deeper than anger, a burning hatred. The anger was understandable, but Murphy couldn't fathom the hatred. Unless he hated Murphy personally—but he didn't know Murphy. Unless he hated the law. Maybe that was it—Young hated the law.

"Surely a hundred dollars would cover the damages and any fine required." Young's voice was smooth now, greasy, as he took five twenties out of his billfold and held them out to Murphy. "I hate to waste the time of going through a court—couldn't I just pay you?"

Murphy looked at the money. The damage in the café was minimal, a tipped table and some stained curtains. Three or four dollars would cover it. The fine was twenty. Here was over a month's wages, just waiting. "Fine will be twenty, another ten to cover damages, and they can walk."

"And cheap at the price," Young pulled the money back, found a ten, and handed over thirty dollars. "Thank you for being so understanding and please accept my apologies. It won't happen again."

Murphy nodded. "I know." He looked at the sun momentarily, then at the dirt, then at Young. "Tell me, Arvis Young, why is it that I don't know you or any of those men? Are you all new in this area?"

Young nodded slowly, showing the same hesitation. "I'm with a mining company from out west. We're thinking of locating in this area to set up operations."

"I thought these mountains were worked out, all the good dirt was gone. . . ."

Again Young nodded. "That's what we hear."

"So you're locating here anyway? In a burned-out mining area?"

A moment, Young smiled. Like a dog chewing meat, the smile. "Well, it will come out later anyway, I suppose, but I wanted to keep it as quiet as I could. The truth is that gold and silver prices are up a bit and my company has patented new mining techniques that make it feasible to reopen a lot of old claims and rework them. We can get pay dirt where no other company can. If it works here, we're going to expand all up and down the front range," he gestured with his arm, "from Denver all the way up into Wyoming."

Murphy had heard all the dreams, all the gimmicks —how hydraulic mining would save the town, how some new chemical would extract more gold, how some new magic would come and start everything up again, restore the old glory—which had never been very glorious in Murphy's eyes—to the mining towns. Dreams. Dust dreams.

"I'll come out and see how it works," Murphy said, not a question, a statement. "Where are you located?"

Something came into Young's eyes. Just for a second there was a flash of something intense, deep— anger? No. Mixed with something else. Anger and fear? Deeper, perhaps—anger and hatred?

"We're west. West of town. But we're not entertaining visitors yet." The same flat statement as Murphy's. Not a question—a telling. Now there was something definite between them, something Murphy could almost smell. Young didn't share, didn't give, didn't take any interference in his affairs. Likewise, Murphy didn't recognize obstacles, went over them, through them, even if they were seemingly insurmountable like Young.

"I'll come anyway. Tomorrow. West, you say?"

"We're really not set up . . ."

"Tomorrow." Murphy kept his voice even, turned, walked away from Young, headed to the jail to release

47

the men. He doubted that any new method could do what Young said it could do, but didn't know enough about mining to speculate. He knew only one thing about Young and the miners: Young was too damn slick with a mean cut in his eyes, and his men had lied, held back.

And he was getting damn sick of being lied to.

CHAPTER 5

IT WAS JUST dawn when Murphy left the edge of town. Midge had wrapped him two sandwiches carefully in waxed paper and had rolled a quart jar of coffee in sacking to hold some of the heat in. He had put the coffee and sandwiches in the saddlebags at the livery. But as soon as he swung a leg over the gray in front of the livery barn, the horse had popped on him, done four or five morning hops to green out before he was truly in the saddle, and Murphy had come down on the sandwiches, crushing them.

By the time he had the gray on the ground, he had bounced across the street and come up under the eaves of the blacksmith shop, crushing his hat and jarring his teeth halfway down his throat.

The froggy horse, coupled with the fact that Murphy really didn't have an idea of where to start or what to do, put him in a surly mood, and he jerked the bit unnecessarily, which made the horse more nervous. As he cleared the back of town, a street dog came out and took a cut at the gray's back feet and again Murphy wound up half in the saddle, at a full gallop, cutting between two houses and scaring the hell out of Moe Harper's chickens.

It had not been a good start.

At the edge of town he stopped, settled the horse, and regained control, also settling his mind. An old cowboy with a face like a tired pair of boots had once told him there was a definite connection between a rider's brain and his behind, and that all his thoughts went through the connection into the horse. The old man had been serious, had spent most of his days and a hell of a lot of his nights on a horse eating cow dust, and really believed in the connection.

Murphy didn't know how the feelings passed to the horse, but they did. A scared rider made a scared horse, a mad rider made a mad horse. Murphy watched the sunrise, sat still until the horse eased down, then let the gray pick his own way west out of town. He felt foolish taking off on the search without having a method in mind, but he had exhausted every other source of information.

It was, he decided when his teeth stopped aching and he had his hat reblocked, a beautiful morning for a ride. To hell with the reason. He was jogging west, and to the rear the sun came up over the prairie, warmed his back, and lighted the mountains in front of him, spread all across the world with a pure, golden light. There was still snow on the high peaks, and the sun turned it a brilliant yellow, so that it seemed the mountains were on fire.

Many times in the years he had been sheriff of Cincherville he had wondered how man could make anything as ugly as this town. Gray, weathered buildings in flat colors, working toward rot; mud in the spring during breakup so deep it went to axle hubs; dust in the summer to fill your nostrils when a freight wagon came through. Outhouses stinking in the summer heat, or worse, buckets of filth just thrown out the back of some buildings in the open where the flies could get at it. Murphy could not believe a man could do anything that ugly and come out every morning and look west and see these mountains.

But it was there, the town. Sitting on the edge of beauty like a wart on a beautiful woman's nose. He looked back down on it as he climbed the hills, saw the smoke coming from Midge's chimney, and thought of the night before. He had stayed when she closed the café and they had talked, really talked, of their future.

Sitting at a table, drinking coffee from the thick mugs Midge had ordered from a supplier in Denver, Murphy had looked down at the oilcloth on the table, covered with small flowers and little green leaves. For a moment then, in the night while she talked, he had imagined that he was somebody else—a worker, a man who had come home after a day working, maybe a hand or a ranch owner, sitting at the table with his lady making plans for the future.

"We could go north," she had said. "Up in Montana there's cheap land and we could start up there. . . ."

He had nodded, thinking with wonder that this was the first time they had truly looked at it. They had known they would do something, had to do something, but they had not specified what, or how. Now she was saying it and he was nodding, and the saying it and agreeing to it made it somehow become real.

They would do this, he felt. The two of them would go when they got a little money, go to Montana and find some cheap land. He had looked up at her and thought how beautiful, how soft and delicate and beautiful she looked in the gentle yellow light from the oil lamp on the table and yet how strong. And the moment had grown until he could see the place they would have in Montana; see it in a small canyon with a log house, log barn, corrals and something young, young calves or chicks and perhaps a kid, see it all in the yellow glow from the lamp on her face, in the curve down to her chin, the strong curve, and he thought he could not love her more or believe in her more than he did.

Then he had looked back down at his hands and had seen the knuckles, all scar tissue and malformed, driven back and in and broken from countless bar fights, countless driving blows and rips and cuts to keep the peace, keep him alive, and he thought that was all he knew. From the gutted Tenderloin of New York where he'd been reared as a whore's son, through the army west, and the law—all he knew was what he did. He had never worked on a ranch, never been a miner, never been a laborer. A soldier and a lawman. When he looked at his hands he could not see how it could work and yet when he looked back up at Midge he could not see how they could fail.

A wonderment. A thing to wonder at, like the mountains on fire that he rode toward now in the cool morning air. He took out the quart jar of coffee—

somehow, miraculously, when he had come down on the sandwiches he had not broken the jar. He sipped some of the strong egg coffee. Midge always boiled coffee grounds in water, with an egg in it to smooth some of the acid and give the coffee a clean taste. It was already cool, but he liked cool coffee as well as hot, and the taste somehow mixed with the morning light and the movement of the gray and he felt light-headed, happy, almost childlike. As if he were going on a picnic or an outing. One of these days he would have to take Midge and head up into the hills for a picnic.

He had been working up a small draw, and at the end there was a low wall of rocks and dirt. The gray scrabbled up, pulling like a cat, and he lifted with his legs and body to help the horse, came out on top of the edge to find himself in scrub brush country—some sage, mostly stunted willow, and something like mesquite that he couldn't name but that burned with a thick, oily smoke when used in a fire.

He still had no real plan. West of town there were many abandoned mines—the hills up toward the mountains were thick with them. Holes dotted every hillside and canyon. Most of them were for nothing, shallow diggings that went in fifty feet and played out. Now and then somebody had hit better dirt and stayed with it a bit longer, so there would be a pile of tailings from the digging, broken rock and shale sliding down the mountain in rubbled heaps. There were almost no good mines. Up near Central City, Idaho Springs, they had hit good dirt, heavy gold and silver, and had a real boom.

Men had come to the area around Cincherville filled with the same enthusiasm, driven by the same greeds and lusts. Find the yellow money, find it all. But Cincherville had been, really, the worst of all possible places to mine—the kind of country that kept teasing and never paid off. Color was found, gold and some silver, lead and lots of quartz—God, the white quartz rocks were everywhere. Murphy had even seen an outhouse made of white quartz cemented together. Enough small veins, little traces, quartz, and lead were found to feed hope to an army of miners—but none of them ever hit the motherlode. There were no bonanzas, no wild strikes, just endless holes in endless mountains and hills, until even those with the deepest hope moved on. Higher into the mountains. Further up the slope. Leaving, always leaving until nothing was left.

Nothing was left for all the sweat and blood, torn muscles and aching bones except the endless holes and shacks, the endless piles of rock and dirt, the rusting machinery.

He had in his mind that he might work up into the Huerfano Canyon area. Straight west of Cincherville, the Huerfano Canyon had been the most promising of the areas that didn't pay off. It was full of old mines, and there were still some of them, spread through the five subcanyons that comprised the whole Huerfano system, where diehards hung on and picked and scraped and tried to find a little dust. Tilman had mentioned that Wangsu had gotten leather to make a harness for a burro. He didn't need a burro for working his garden, and it wasn't like Wangsu to keep an animal, feed an animal he wasn't going to use. One of the ladies in the town had mentioned that she had seen Wangsu leading a burro west of town with a pack one morning, and Murphy thought there might be a chance he was carrying eggs or vegetables into the Huerfano to sell to the miners.

It was a faint chance, but a start. The region was fifteen miles out, too far for them to get into town often, and Wangsu might have thought it a way to make some more money.

Sketchy. Pulling at straw, he thought, heeling the gray into a light canter. The horse had a bitch trot, shook his guts out, and it would smooth the trot if taken up into a canter and brought back down, rather than just go up through a walk. He held the center for half a mile, across the flat he was on, then down into a draw that became a trail to the Huerfano River, a dry bed that flowed wet in spring out of the canyon.

Part of the problem with Wangsu going into the Huerfano was that it was so isolated. There were several men in there who could not be with people, could not be in the light, who had to live in places that were isolated. Murphy knew of them, knew that there was paper on some of them from things back East, but stayed away as long as things were running smoothly.

Arvis Young had been right. Miners were rough people, men who could not stay in the East and live, men who had no more smooth edges than the rocks they tore out of the ground. They were bad enough. Murphy had seen the good ones, the ones who could come to town, had seen them when they were not truly human; had seen them gouge each other's eyes out, cripple each other, cut and kill each other over a place to stand at the bar.

And those were the good ones. The bad ones, the men who could not be with people, were back in the Huerfano running the dead mines—there were some of them worth only the killing. And that's what it came down to. They would not argue, not stick to the rules that worked for normal people—men like these killed first. Before all things they killed. Murphy had only once before been into the Huerfano. He had followed a killer named Fessel back in, a wild man who had gunned down two men in the saloon for no apparent reason other than boredom and had ridden out of town on a stolen horse. Murphy had ridden after him, up the draws and into the Huerfano, and found him waiting in the settlement—four shacks in the same clearing. There had been three other men there but they hadn't wanted any of it, and when Fessel had taken a shot at Murphy, the sheriff had returned the fire, emptying his cylinder, and Fessel was dead when he hit the ground. Getting out of Huerfano had been tight—men came from their holes to watch him, some with rifles in their hands, but they had let him pass.

Considering what the Huerfano was, it seemed unlikely that Wangsu had gone there to sell. But he had gone west with a burro packed, and that was all that lay west. Murphy could also use the trip to check on Arvis Young's so-called operation—which stunk to high heaven. He would smell around in the Huerfanos and if nothing panned there—he smiled when he thought of the humor of nothing *panning* in that busted canyon—he would check the McCormick hole south down the face of the foothills, spend the night there, and call it good.

What he was beginning to suspect was that somebody had killed Wangsu. The reason wasn't important. There were men who hated the Chinese for no reason, men who thought they were taking the work, men who hated them for their pigtails or their clothes or eyes. One of them could have seen Wangsu walking out here and shot him out of hand; shot him for the burro, his shoes, for what he had in his pocket. If that had happened, Murphy would probably not find the body—by now the coyotes and buzzards would have it—and there would never be an answer to the questions.

Questions.

What would Wangsu be doing with the store owner —maybe the rest of the town—to make the owner lie that way? If he weren't selling vegetables, what was he doing heading toward the Huerfano with a burro and a pack?

It was the questions that saved Murphy's life. He reached up to ease his hatband, thinking, wiping the sweat off, and he fumbled with the hat and dropped it. The hat started to fall to the ground and he hunched down quickly to get it and in that split second it sounded like the whole side of the canyon had exploded.

There were two, maybe three rifles up on the right side of the canyon in back of the rocks, and they had been shooting for the man. Murphy heard two snaps as bullets passed where his body had been, then the sound of the rifles; the high crack came across. And more cracks, almost at once. He felt the gray take two solid hits in the body—one in the lungs, because the wind whistled out of him—and start down, and Murphy continued his leaning motion and fell out of the saddle to the ground as the gray nosed over, dying.

Murphy hit the dirt rolling, over on one shoulder, then up and running for some large boulders on his right. He heard more snaps as they shot around him, but no hits, he felt no hits, and he threw himself down in back of one of the boulders.

He had temporary cover. Breathing room. A bullet hit near his boots, which were out a bit, and he pulled them in. Now they simply shot around the boulder, putting slugs into the rocks and dirt to keep him down, and Murphy swung his eyes, looking for a hole, a way out. He was in a rocky basin with no other cover save some brush and more boulders all the way across the other side. In the middle of the small basin the gray lay kicking and dying, its head thrashing against the ground.

Damn.

Sitting there, riding into the Huerfano and I was sitting there like a craphead—not thinking.

More shots now, cutting the air around him, but they couldn't get at him just yet. They would have to keep him pinned, and one or two of them could move off to the side to get a clear shot at him. Then it was just a matter of time until they got one in him and he joined the gray. He wished he'd brought a rifle. He had thought of it but changed his mind because he hated to ride with it sticking under his leg. If he had a rifle he could at least shoot back. They sounded to be eighty, ninety yards away. With his Smith he might as well throw rocks.

Another look. I'm like a spider in a washbasin, he thought.

I could die here.

CHAPTER 6

Bullets.

God, he couldn't believe the bullets they had—they must have boxes of the damn things. Murphy hunkered in the low spot near the bottom of the boulder, holding the Smith ineffectively in one hand.

There were three of them, he was certain of it now. Two of them were firing a steady pattern at and around his boulder, and they were good. Slugs tore the earth near him, skinning the edge of the rock by hairs. He had pulled his legs in but not before one near miss had creased his boot top, and another nearly closed his right eye when he stole a quick look to try and locate the rifles.

The two shooters kept him pinned, and he guessed the third one was working off to the side, staying high, to get a clear shot at him. He knew he was running out of time. Minutes now, maybe seconds. He looked around the basin again, trying to find cover, and there was nothing. Nothing.

Except the gray.

The dead horse lay forty feet away, already starting to draw flies. Forty feet to the horse, then another fifty feet to the rocks at the side of the basin opposite the attackers. It might as well be fifty miles. Lead smacked near his right ear, a new shot from the side. His choices were diminishing fast. The third man had moved a hundred feet and more, and had a new angle. Still not quite enough to finish Murphy off, but close. And in a few more seconds he would have the angle, and Murphy would be a clear target. . . .

No, he had to move and move fast and move right. Again he looked to the gray, to the horse and the flies. He mentally rehearsed his movements; forty feet, then down—ten, twelve steps and down, then roll, up and fifteen, no, twenty more steps and dive into the rocks. Right. And the world rides on the back of a big turtle. There was no chance, unless . . .

He looked around the boulder again, drew three fast shots. If he could draw them out a bit, get them to shoot fast and have to reload. Maybe. Maybe.

Murphy put his head out to the left of the boulder and drew it back, taking three quick rounds; then the other side, two more; one more duck and five shots. He swung the Smith around the edge of the rock and fired six shots up in the general direction of the mountain and was up and running.

But his plan didn't work—they were pouring it down on him now. Dirt spurted up all around him as he ran, and he felt the spot on his back, the tiny spot where he was certain the bullets would hit him, would pound into him. Quickly, he dived and was behind the gray. Three, four more slugs tore into the dead horse—Murphy felt the carcass jolt with the impact.

"I hit him!" A hoarse voice came down. "I know I hit the son of a bitch just before he got to the horse." Another voice cut in, "You didn't hit squat—he was jumping."

Murphy took four deep breaths, kept from springing until he was ready—they were shooting into the horse now, trying to get slugs through it and into him. Another breath, then roll and up and run—run for all that was in him, his legs pumping, driving the word RUN-RUN-RUN and he was there, almost there. He was going to make it through the snapping storm of lead; he was almost there, four steps to go . . . three . . . two . . . and one . . . and the slug took him. It drove him down, spinning. He was hit. Just above the right hip, in the soft meat, a grazing blow took him, and the hydraulic shock of the bullet stunned his whole side into numbness for part of a second as he spun to the left and fell down.

He landed in some small rocks, jamming his head into a rock and knocking his hat off, coming down hard on his shoulder. Like a crab, he scuttled ahead into some slightly larger rocks, and was amazed to find that with all his size he could flatten low enough to find cover behind them.

Murphy raised slightly up and looked down at his side. The bullet had torn across and made a nasty, ripped gouge but seemed to have missed anything vital. Except my meat, he thought—which was vital enough. Pain came as he looked, working in dull, then hot waves from the wound up his side and into his brain.

"That time I know I hit him!" somebody yelled. "It was a clean shot, and I saw the dust fly off his shirt. Saw blood too. I tell you I hit him."

A pause, then a second voice. "I think he's right—I saw the blood too."

Another time passed, perhaps a minute, and Murphy carefully reloaded the Smith from his belt loops, trying not to show any movement around the rocks. He was in a much better place now, with good rocks on all sides, although they were not as big as he would have wished. Wished, he thought—if he were wishing, he would wish for a detachment of cavalry to ride in about now. Maybe with Gatling guns. But the cover was good here, much better, and he might be able to work back through the rocks and get away. They couldn't get around in back of him. . . .

"You figure he's dead?"

This was the first voice again, and Murphy thought: No, I can't be that lucky.

"I don't know. I saw the hit, looked like it was low in the back. A solid hit. He's probably dead."

"You want to go back and tell the boss that?"

A long pause. "You mean without checking?"

"That's what I mean—you want to do that and then find out he wasn't dead? The boss will make harness leather out of your back. You saw what he could do with a knife."

Come on, Murphy thought, come down and look. If

they would just come within pistol range, just come on, come on. The pain in his side roared through him now, and he wished he could move and compress his bandana or part of his shirt in the wound, but he was afraid if he moved that much they would see it. A fly landed on his hand and he watched it crawl. In the silence—the first silence since they had begun firing —he heard birds singing. How could they be singing? Some kind of desert bird, maybe a desert lark—there were many larks to sing. The gunfire hadn't bothered them. His brain was getting fuzzy with wound shock and he fought to bring his thoughts back to sanity. He wanted to be clear-headed. . . .

"Go down there and check it out."

Ahh, Murphy thought. He eased the hammer back on the Smith, had the first round ready.

"To hell with that. You go down."

"I'm not the one who says I hit him. You go down and we'll cover you. If you're so sure you hit him, what are you afraid of?"

"Oh, hell then, give me some cover." And with further grumbling and swearing he started to move. Murphy could hear the rocks fall as he stumbled, working slowly down the side of the canyon.

Have to be patient, Murphy thought. Like waiting for antelope. Just wait, and wait and wait and wait . . . easy down, easy down.

He could not see anything, had to go by sound, and the man moved slowly, so slowly. He watched the fly on his hand, listened to the birds and the man moving, kicking rocks, working down the hill, and finally into the sand of the basin. Still too far, too far. He wanted him to come close, no chance to miss.

"What do you think?" One of the men who stayed high called down. "Is he dead?"

"I can't tell yet—can't see him. Hold your horses. Let me work past the horse, then I'll go off to the side and see if I can get another slug in him. We'll just make sure. . . ."

Still too far, Murphy thought. He held his breath, listening with all that he was, hearing the sound of the man's feet in the sand—almost impossible to hear anything. Murphy would have to make his move soon, before the man could get a shot at him. But where was he? At the horse? No, maybe just past the horse, to the left of the dead horse, maybe there.

"I see him now, I see part of his hand. . . ."

Murphy rolled and came up, fighting the sudden explosion of pain in his side. He swung the Smith over the rock in front of him, brought his head up, and there he saw—standing between the horse and himself, holding a rifle—a man with a flat miner's hat and white-wide eyes. Fear eyes, startled eyes.

Murphy squeezed off a round, saw dust puff off the man's shirt, then pulled three more as fast as he could. He didn't wait to see if the last three hit, just fell back under the rock as the whole world blew up. Both rifles up on the canyon side opened and tore at the rock, but he was down and safe. They couldn't hit him now and he was sure he had taken the one man out. The bullet struck near the center of the chest, and he was certain the man would not get up to fire again.

The two remaining attackers kept up a steady fire for a time. Fifteen, twenty, perhaps thirty rounds hit around his hiding place—he was again amazed at the number of bullets they had. They must have planned on a big gun battle, planned on needing a lot of ammunition.

He worked on his side now. He always wore a bandana to cover his mouth when the dust got bad. He took it off, made a rectangle out of it, and placed it along the wound. He had no tape but his belt—not his gunbelt but his regular belt—was made of soft leather, and he pulled it out of the pants loops and moved it higher, to cover the bandana and wound, and refastened it, pulling it as tight as he could to make a compress on the wound and stop the bleeding, which had already abated somewhat.

Twice he nearly passed out. The pain had gone from the white flash of a new wound to a duller but deeper, more lasting throb. Still the shock came in smaller waves, weakening him and making him dizzy. When he had the wound bound he lay back, raised his feet a bit, and propped them on a small rock, breathing deeply.

His situation was better, but still bad. They held high ground, there were two of them and they had rifles. He was wounded, on low ground, and had only a handgun. On the plus side, he had good cover and they didn't dare come down to him. If they tried to work around him now, it wouldn't do any good because he had decent cover on all sides. The way it looked was they could stay and wait him out, hoping for a clear shot (which wasn't going to happen—he wasn't about to give them a clear shot), or they could get the hell out. Or, he thought, smiling tightly, they could surrender.

Not likely.

A stalemate.

They had stopped firing again, and he could hear them talking, although he couldn't hear well enough to make out what they were saying, except in snatches.

"Carl dead . . . no, leave him . . . can't do anything now . . ."

Then some falling rocks and nothing. Two minutes, three, five, and finally ten. He heard some horses moving up the canyon, riding away, and still he waited. If they were truly gone, a wait wouldn't hurt. If they were tricking him, waiting could save his life.

When a full thirty minutes were gone and he had heard nothing he raised his head quickly, and dropped it. Nothing. He did it again, held it up for a while, saw no movement in the rocks above, and decided they were gone. He rose to his knees and, propping himself on the rock, pulled himself to his feet.

His side tore at him. For a second he thought he was going to fall, pass out, but he quickly began to feel more steady. He waited another minute, watching the rocks and remaining ready to drop at the first sign of movement. When nothing came he stepped— staggered—out to the dead man on the ground.

Murphy had hit him twice. Once in the center of the chest, the next one in the right shoulder. He was lying face up—had fallen straight back with the bullets— and Murphy went through his pockets. Nothing to identify him. A twenty-dollar gold eagle in one pocket, some tobacco in another. In a pouch around his neck there were thirty or more bullets—.44-40—for the rifle he had dropped in the dirt. Murphy picked the rifle up and blew sand out of the action, then took the bullet pouch. If they came back he would be ready for them.

He went to the bullet-riddled gray and dug in the saddlebags. He had not been lucky with the coffee this time. The jar had broken when the horse went down. But it had broken off at the top and there were still close to two cups of coffee in the broken bottom. He drank it carefully, avoiding cutting himself or swallowing any chips of glass. He had lost blood and needed the fluid—especially the coffee jolt. Doc Hensley told him once they used coffee to fight wound shock in the Civil War—made a thick coffee they put in wounded men with enemas. Something in the coffee kept them out of shock, and Murphy would need all the help he could get.

He was going to have to walk eight, nine miles with his side on fire. But at least his legs worked. He looked again at the dead man and thought that they might have left his horse where they had their own tied, but decided that was pushing luck. They would have taken it or at least cut it loose, and Murphy didn't have the strength to be heading off in the wrong direction chasing a horse around.

He started walking. One step in front of the next, headed back down-canyon toward Cincherville. A world, a lifetime away.

If the wound opened, he could bleed out. If he passed out, he could die of thirst before somebody found him. He would need luck now.

All the luck there was.

CHAPTER 7

IT PROVED TO be a long walk.

He had walked miles before, of course—when they gulled him into joining the army back in New York, still full of piss and vinegar, and young and stupid enough to believe the recruiter's lies about seeing new country and fighting the savages. He had joined the cavalry but had spent the first three months walking. They had shipped him to Fort Leavenworth, Kansas —it was just after the Civil War—and he had walked until he'd worn out his riding boots. Miles and miles, carrying a .45-70 trapdoor rifle, walking and walking.

But not like this.

Murphy figured he'd come about nine miles from town by mid-morning when the three men had started shooting at him. It was around noon when it was over and Murphy had started to walk toward town. He guessed it might take him four or five hours to walk back to town.

Inside of ten steps his body told him how wrong that was. The bullet had cut across the muscles that went down his side, and he had not realized how important a part those muscles played in walking, just walking.

The top was connected to the bottom, and somehow when his right leg moved forward, no matter how much he tried to control the action, it pulled directly on the muscles damaged by the bullet.

It was agony, like somebody twisting a knife in his side.

He tried walking while leaning over to the right, tried clamping the muscles with his elbow, tried loosening the belt over the wound, tightening it, limping, not limping, swearing. Nothing helped.

Finally he came up with a kind of limp-stagger-shuffle, dragging his right foot. That seemed to work best but it cut him down in speed to where he was fortunate to make the first mile in an hour and a half. Often he stopped to lean against rocks. Once he sat in the shade of some brush for half an hour.

Halfway through the second mile his brain went—whether from shock or the pain or a mixture of both—and he couldn't control his thoughts. They went out ahead of him like wisps, the thoughts.

Should have loosened the cinch on the gray—not good to leave a horse cinched like that for a long time in the sun. Had an uncle who did that once and when he got back on the horse it frogged on him and broke his arm. Old man had to wear a cast for months. Should have loosened the cinch. Don't want a broken arm . . .

He would shake his head and his mind would clear, then the fog would return and he would dream again. He thought he heard horses running, heard their hooves in the dirt. Could have sworn the two men were coming back for him, looking for him.

He spent close to an hour hiding in back of some rocks with the Smith out—he had long before dropped the rifle—waiting for them.

But it was nothing, nothing, and he started walking again.

All through the afternoon, the heat cooking him, in and out of hallucinations, in and out of shock, step-shuffle-drag-limp, he worked down the canyons until it was dark, hard dark, and still he went. He did not think any longer of where he was going or where he had been. There was only the step, just the next step, and then the next and one more . . .

When at last he came out on the road that went west of Cincherville, a mile now from town, it was three in the morning and cooling, and he was not human anymore. He staggered the last mile on some reflex, falling forward until he came to Doc's door, where he knocked. He must have pounded because as he was falling, with his face sliding down the door to lie in a crumpled heap, as he was falling, he saw somebody light a lamp in the back, the yellow light flickering out and out, and then there was nothing.

Everything was bright.

The brightness went inside his eyes through closed lids, into his head, cut to the center of his brain, and he opened his eyes, squinting, trying to stop the brightness.

Doc was holding a mirror, catching window sun and flashing it in his eyes. He was in the back room at Doc Hensley's, everything white and clean and bright. God, for the light. He closed his eyes, opened them again. "That's enough . . ."

Doc put the mirror down. "Didn't mean to wake you. I had to check your eyes to make sure there were no head injuries."

"How long have I been here—out?"

"Two days, a bit more. You came in about four Wednesday morning, it's Friday now. Mid-morning. How are you feeling?"

"Wonderful." Murphy started to rise, felt his side blow up, and fell back. "God."

Doc nodded. "You won't be moving like that for a few more days." He brought some coffee and held Murphy's head up, helping him sip. "I didn't try to bring you around sooner because I wanted you out while I worked on your side. It was a clean wound but the bullet carried some of your shirt in with it, then you had to make it worse by tying an old hanky in there—hell, you're lucky you didn't get gangrene."

"I was bleeding . . ."

"I shouldn't wonder. Bullets do that. Here, I've got some soup Midge left for you. Try to get as much fluid in as possible, coffee and soup. You lost some blood and a lot of sweat."

"Midge. Is she all right?"

"She's not the one who got shot."

"I know, but worry. She'll worry."

Doc nodded again. "I called her to help. You were crazy for a while and she helped me hold you down while I worked on you. Then she sat all night the first night and most of the second. We weren't sure you were going to pull through."

"Where is she now?"

"I told her to go sleep but if I know her, she's opened the café and is serving—whole damn town nearly starved because of you." He mumbled as he worked, lifting the dressing on the wound. "Good. Looks clean now, and the redness is going away. I don't even think it's infected. A miracle, really, figuring the way you treated it."

"I have to get up."

"Well, now, that's a whole new thing—you have to get up. You might *want* to, you might think you *have* to, but I promise you if you do, you're going to fall flat on your face. I don't care how much of a hero you think you are."

"No." Murphy shook his head. "Not a hero—I have to go to the bathroom."

"Oh." Doc helped him with a pan and Murphy used it, hating the helpless feeling. As weak as a kitten, all of him, soft and weak. "When can I ride?" he asked after he was through.

Doc snorted. "Ride, hell, ask when you can sit up, walk. I don't know about riding. Two weeks, at least, maybe a month. Is there a hurry?"

Murphy thought about the canyon, the gray falling beneath him, the bullets—the damn bullets—and the two men who got away. "Yes. There's a hurry. I've got to see a couple of men . . ."

"What happened out there?"

Murphy lay back on the bed and thought. "I can't remember all of it yet, but most of it . . ." He told Doc what he could remember, leaving out nothing, tried to remember how far it was, what side canyon it was near.

"Your saddle is still there," Doc said, when he'd finished. "I'll get somebody and go up to get the body and your gear off the horse. Can we get a wagon up there?"

Murphy shook his head. "They'll have to use packs. It's up in those trails, too narrow for a wagon."

"I'll take care of it. You drink more soup and rest. I'm going to tell Midge you're all right. Just lie back and sleep if you can."

Hensley left then, and his back no sooner cleared the door than Murphy's brain started chewing on what had happened, and as soon as he started to think, it poured in—all end over end and upside down, or so it seemed. He tried to sort it out.

Three men had laid for him, had just about taken him out—they had planned it, planned specifically on ambushing him; with pouches of bullets around their necks, with rifles, in a place where they should have, would have been able to get him clean if he hadn't been lucky.

They had laid for him, and if it had just been rawhiders, just the men who could not be with people, they wouldn't have been prepared, wouldn't have been expecting him. . . . Who knew he was riding west? He hadn't told anybody—how could they have known? And what about Wangsu? Were the two things unrelated?

He closed his eyes and the thoughts clouded over, mixed, and rolled and he went under again, only this time to sleep. To rest.

When his eyes opened again it was dark outside and

the lamp on the white table in the corner was lighted. Midge was sitting near him, sewing something, and he studied her for a moment before she knew he was awake. She had lines under her eyes from crying and staying awake, and he thought he should tell her how he was feeling, how much he loved her, but instead he said, simply, "Hello."

She started and stood and came to him, put her hand on his, and smiled. "It's good, really good to see you awake." Murphy looked at her and his throat filled but he said nothing.

"I was worried," she said, squeezing his hand, "worried that you . . . well, just worried."

He smiled. "I don't figure to get my ticket punched just yet. . . ."

They quit talking then, and didn't speak any further but sat in the yellow light until he dozed off again. When he came up the next time she was gone but he still felt her there and it was daylight again and he was sick of being down.

The sun was streaming in the window but he was alone. Next to the bed on a stand was a small pot with coffee in it, cold, but he poured some in a cup, his hand shaking, and grimaced as he drank it down. It tasted like tar, and in fact his mouth felt like tar— thick and gummy. He rubbed his cheek and felt stubble.

And he was suddenly, deeply, intensely hungry; as if he hadn't eaten anything in his whole life. Starving. He sat up slowly, felt the pulling in his side, the pain, but fought it and kept moving until he was sitting straight.

"Unnngh." It slipped out without his meaning it, a

low sound, and he sat for a bit until the pulling and pain went down. Doc said weeks, but Murphy didn't have weeks. It figured that he maybe didn't have days—and he'd been on his back for two—no, three days already.

He had to get his strength back, had to carry it back to them, find them, and carry it back. If he stayed on his back and waited, whoever it was might come to finish the job. He had to get up, be on his feet. When the pain eased, he put his feet square, braced with one hand on the end of the bed, and stood up.

He was wobbly and his legs started to sag. He fought the pain and weakness but started down, and then came back up, hanging on the bed.

"What in hell are you doing?" Doc came storming in. He was dressed for outside, for riding. "Are you out of your damn mind? I told you to take it easy and here you're trying to stand up."

Murphy turned slowly, but remained standing. "I can't stay down. They might come for me. I have to get back up." He was weak, and when he tried to take a step he almost collapsed. "Help me."

Doc stepped forward, took Murphy's arm, and helped him back to the bed. "You're talking crazy—they won't come for you here. I won't let them."

Murphy shook his head. "You don't understand all the things that are happening. It wasn't just a bunch of rawhiders or riders—this was a setup. And there is another side—Wangsu is missing, and I was looking for him. Somehow I think there is something linking everything together. I have to get back on my feet and you have to help me."

Doc took his coat off, hung it up, and turned back to

76

Murphy. "You're serious, aren't you? You really think I can just give you a pill or something and it will all go away, don't you?"

Murphy looked at him, said nothing.

"Well, I can't. You have to heal."

Still Murphy said nothing. Talk didn't change anything. It never did.

"Your body has to heal, heal itself . . . ahh, hell, get up on the table." He went to the glass chest on the wall and found several rolls of tape and gauze. "You're worse than those kids in the war. Get blown all to hell and then want me to sew it back on so they can get back into the fighting. Had any goddamn brains you'd take that woman and get the hell out of here, that's what you'd do."

There was more but Doc's words were lost in mumbling, and Murphy smiled as he shuffled slowly to the metal table in the examining room. Doc would get the job done. He might gripe but he always got it done. Murphy turned backward and sat up on the edge of the table. He was still terribly weak, but he could feel his legs gaining strength.

Doc raised his arm slowly until the elbow was low and out to the side. "Hold it like that, steady."

He lifted the old gauze off the wound, giving a savage snort when it stuck and Murphy grunted. "Looks all right. Of course you'll probably tear it and bleed to death. Damn fool. Here, hold your arm up and steady like this." He pushed the arm into position and held it to show what he wanted. Then he lay a new gauze pad over the wound and began taping, all around Murphy's waist. Binding him was an involved job—Doc took the tape up and over the shoulder, pulled the arm down, and taped the upper arm into position—and when it was done Murphy felt like he'd been rolled in a rug.

"I can't move my upper arm." He pulled, tried to raise it, couldn't.

"That's right. You're not supposed to be able to move it. I had to immobilize it and keep it solid or you'd tear that wound open. You got away with it once, but the next time you could get infected and that will do you. You understand?"

"I can move? I can ride?"

"Not unless you're a damn fool—which I guess you must be. If you move, move slowly, evenly, don't jerk the left arm or shoulder. And if you ride, for God's sake get a slow horse and don't push it. Let your body talk to you . . . listen to it."

Murphy nodded and stood—with even, measured movements. His legs felt to be half rubber. He thought for a moment that he didn't have a shirt but Doc pulled one out of a bag—he'd gone to the hotel and gotten clothes from Murphy's room.

"Oh, I almost forgot. Wayne and I took a packhorse out and got your saddle. The gray was still there, and the saddle, but the body was gone."

"Gone?"

Doc nodded. "They must have come back for him later. You're lucky they didn't come on after you."

Murphy nodded, thinking. The way he was stumbling, walking, falling, they could have had him for the asking. "You brought the saddle back, you say?"

"It's at the livery, with the rest of your tack. Perhaps of medical interest—I counted sixteen bullet holes in the gray and that was just from a cursory examination."

"They shot after the horse was down, when I was in back of it." Murphy swore. "Help me with this shirt, will you? I can't get my arm through the sleeve."

Doc helped him dress, and when he was done Murphy strapped his gun belt on, checked the Smith to be sure it was loaded, then moved slowly to the door.

"Where are you going?"

"To Midge's. I'm going to eat everything in the kitchen. Then I'm going to have a drink. Then I've got to see a man about a horse. . . ."

He walked out into the sun.

CHAPTER 8

MURPHY WAS SITTING at Midge's, eating a second helping of kitchen stew—she always had a pot of either pinto beans or kitchen stew, with whatever she had left over from the day before, sitting on the back of the stove to stay warm. Miners usually wanted it fast and they wanted it plentiful, so she kept the pot ready for sudden orders.

The stew was just what Murphy needed. The first helping filled him out and the second seemed to go into his legs and arms, giving strength. He drank three cups of coffee and was just finishing when two men came in and sat down near the table. He knew them slightly from some trouble with a horse. Couldn't remember their names, but remembered the problem. One of them had sold a horse to the other but had not been paid in full. There came a day when they were both drunk in the saloon and the unpaid money for the horse had turned into one hell of a fight. Murphy had been called to settle it, and when he walked in, both of them stopped fighting, just like that, and asked him politely if he would stay out of this if they went outside and settled it.

They had been so polite, just like a couple of little boys, that he had nodded and they took it outside and tore up half the street. Eventually both of them were on their knees, slamming at each other, when Murphy once more stepped in and stopped it. Then they had stood, shook hands with each other and with Murphy and all the men from the saloon who had come outside to watch. They explained that they were brothers and always settled their differences this way, thank you, and the drinks were on them.

They nodded to Murphy and ordered some stew and started talking. Murphy emptied his coffee and stood to leave, slowly, when one of the brothers held up a hand.

"Sheriff, you got a minute?"

Murphy nodded and walked to their table. "What's the matter?"

The brother shrugged. "Probably nothing. We were riding out on that rim country north and west of town—up there by those old mines on the ridge where that fire went through. You know where I mean?"

Murphy thought. "Yeah—I used to hunt up there once in a while. There were some early fall elk that used to be there. Before everybody shot them out."

"Yeah, up there. We were riding up there and had started back when we saw a bunch of buzzards up on the north side, where that mesa starts. They seemed to be flying around a bunch of tailings up back by some old shacks, but we didn't have time to ride over to check it out. It was coming on dark and we had a load anyway. . . ."

"Load of what?"

"Oh, old lumber. We've been going to the old mines around and getting lumber to sell here in town. It pays better than looking at dirt. Anyway we saw those buzzards and thought you might like to know . . ."

Murphy thanked them, thanked Midge for the food, and went outside again. He was noticeably improving. Whether it was the food or the rest or both, he could feel his body coming around, and he stopped on the boardwalk and straightened his belt.

He thought of the buzzards. It was west and a little north of where he had run into the trouble. It might be they had taken the body of the man he'd shot up there to dump it. Not a lot of sense to that, but it was a possibility. There was also the burro that Wangsu had been leading. And there was Wangsu himself, for that matter. It was worth checking out, which brought up the next problem.

He needed a horse.

He lumbered up the street to the livery and found Wayne cleaning a back stall. Murphy was still uncomfortable in the stable. Sarah's body had been found there, in the very stall Wayne was cleaning, and there was still a gouge through one of the poles holding the roof up where Hardesty had tried to hit him with the bull gun.

"I put your saddle and tack in the tack room." Wayne looked up. "I used soil oil on the saddle and tried to work the bloodstain out but it didn't help much."

"Thanks." Murphy fished a dollar out of his pants and threw it to Wayne. "For the trouble."

Wayne handed the money back. "Not for this. This was help, not business. That's different."

Murphy took the dollar. Wayne was a nice kid, liked to be liked. "So we'll do a little business. I'm kind of out of touch—do you have a horse I can rent?"

Wayne jammed the fork in the ground and leaned on the handle. "Well, yes. I've got a couple. I've got a sorrel that isn't too bad and is easy to ride but doesn't have bottom. He won't last if you need him for anything hard. . . ."

He was fishing. Everybody in town knew what had happened, just as they knew they would never hear any details from Midge or Doc. But Wayne was worried about people liking him, and if he could find anything to get some attention he would use it.

"I need something with bottom. I've got to do a little riding. But I don't want anything too froggy, either."

And so it went, back and forth, until Wayne came up with a bay that was a compromise. It was good size, fifteen hands, and wasn't blown but had weak front legs and wouldn't take a long, hard run. It was an easy horse, had been broken gently, and would stand for mounting without any jumping, even in the morning.

They struck a deal. Murphy would rent the horse, look at buying it in the long run, and use it as his own until he bought it or until the rental deal was done.

An hour later he was riding out of town. Saddling had been hard. Wayne had tried to help but Murphy wouldn't let him. Using only his right arm, Murphy had thrown the saddle over the bay and cinched it.

The bridle, oddly enough, was harder because he couldn't raise his left arm high enough to hold it up. But the bay did have a mellow temperament, as Wayne had said, and it was almost helpful.

Murphy pulled himself up with effort, rode to his office, and dismounted, using only his right arm. Inside the office he got a rifle and scabbard—the lever .45-70—and put them on the saddle after loading the magazine. He took ten extra shells and put them in the saddlebag. Discomfort or not, he would not ride without a long gun again.

The rim country was about six miles out, north of the Huerfano Canyon opening in the mountains, and he let the bay make its own way on the trail. It was about noon, and the sun felt good on his left side—it didn't hurt to ride—and he let his eyes work the country ahead and above carefully. He could close his eyes and still remember the sound of the bullets hitting the gray, and he wasn't about to be caught again.

About three o'clock he came up on the rim and saw—about half a mile distant—the shacks the brother had been talking about. There was one buzzard flying over them, not circling but flying past, and Murphy looked for others. Like anything else, they came to feed. One meant nothing. Sometimes a dead horse or cow would bring eight or ten in, especially if it was warm, but one flying past was nothing. As he got closer he saw another one take off, flying heavily, and knew then there was something.

He held up when still out about a hundred yards, could see something on the ground but didn't want to ride into anything. He pulled the Smith—still thinking of the Huerfano—and let the bay walk slowly forward.

The thing on the ground had been a burro. More than buzzards had been at it. Probably coyotes. The main part of the body was gone, even the bones broken apart, and the head was mostly eaten. He could see remnants of a pack on the ground and a halter on the half-eaten head.

Murphy holstered the Smith and swung off the bay, tied it off to the side of a shed and went to the burro. Flies rose in a cloud as he approached. He couldn't tell what had killed it—there wasn't enough left for that—but when he got close to the head and could see the halter he saw strange marks in the leather and realized they were Chinese writing.

He scanned the ground, saw nothing more, then pulled the Smith again and started looking into the shacks. There were five of them, old cabins and lean-tos; miners who used to work nearby probably had built them because they needed a place to sleep. All of the structures were caving in, with no doors, but the wood was weathered and sound so they somehow remained standing. Murphy found Wangsu in the fourth shack.

Or what was left of Wangsu.

The body was tied into an old chair, still upright, but the flies had been at it and Murphy could not look at it long without becoming ill. In the first glance Murphy could tell two things. Wangsu had been stripped and he had been tortured. They had used a knife and . . .

He turned away and went out into the air. So. So damn it, anyway. Damn it all anyway. He pulled air along the sides of his tongue several times to control his stomach, looked at the mountains, then went back in the shack. The smell was as thick as the flies and he held his breath as he examined the body.

Slow cuts, long cuts. Wangsu had died over a long time. There was nothing else in the room, nothing to see except a bootprint in a bloodstain. But there was nothing special about the print, no marks to it, and he went outside again for air.

Why?

That cut through it all. Why do this to Wangsu? What could he have done to make men act like this? Or was it just rawhiders . . . ? No. Not this time. Too much of this was hanging together. Wangsu had something to do with the rest of whatever was going on around here. They had a reason to do this to him. Or thought they had.

He went back into the shack and cut the ropes holding the small figure in the chair. Wangsu only came up to Murphy's mid-chest. Wangsu used to walk along beside him, short and strong.

Perhaps his strength, his ability to put other men in the dirt, had angered some people so much they could do this.

The body fell, slid to the floor. Murphy had a slicker on the saddle and he brought it in, rolled the body in the slicker, and thought about tying it on the horse but figured the bay would probably come apart on him.

Damn. That a thing like this could happen. Wangsu was always smiling.

Murphy decided to make a travois and skid Wangsu home. He found some dry poles and wire and took half an hour to rig up a travois back from the saddle on the bay. The horse stood for it, kicked once but didn't mean it, and Murphy carried out Wangsu's body wrapped in the slicker and tied it to the travois with wire.

The smell had the bay a little worried but the horse settled when Murphy swung on and they started back.

A long ride.

Later, later when there was time, he would sit with Midge in the café and talk of Wangsu and they would drink coffee and he would be surprised at the depth of grief he felt at Wangsu's death; later, when there was time, he would talk to Midge of how strong Wangsu was and how gentle and how he could make things grow where nobody else could make things grow. When there was time he would tell Midge of how he had thought of Wangsu on the long ride home and of how much honor Wangsu had and, finally, how that was all he wanted for himself and Midge—what Wangsu had, a small place and everything neat and clean and settled with no guns. No more guns.

It was a long ride.

CHAPTER 9

MURPHY KNEELED AT the low table, still, with his hands on his legs. In front of him on the table was a steaming clay pot of tea and the same two cups he had seen before. The cups were lacquered and delicate and he noticed now that they had little flowers painted in tracery on the side and he wondered why he hadn't seen the flowers the first time he had been at the table. More came out each time he visited Wangsu, more to see and learn each time. No, there was no more Wangsu to visit, to see. Wangsu was cut-up meat buried in the ground.

Ahh, hell . . . he closed his eyes for a moment. Small pain in his side now, small pain from the wound, and the pulling was nearly gone. But there was still a tightness there. In the wound and in his mind. With his eyes closed, the memory of the long ride came back.

* * *

All the way back to town, the bay walked, pulling the body wrapped in a slicker as the flies buzzed and followed in a cloud, mile after mile until Murphy pulled up in back of Doc's.

Doc Hensley had come out, looked inside the slicker and swore as he dropped the corner back over the body. "Awful, just awful . . ." He found a sheet in the office, a clean white sheet, and they wrapped the body, still in the slicker, in the linen and carried it in to the table. Then Murphy had ridden out to get Tonsun.

She had known when he rode up. She had been in the garden working and she looked up at him when he came. Wearing a conical straw hat, blue pants and tunic, she had stood with the hoe in her hands and looked at Murphy and known—she had known why he was there before he spoke. Her body had wilted. She didn't go down, didn't get hysterical, didn't break but she knew; it was like something went out of her, flying out and away from her. She carefully put the hoe in the rack in the corner of the garden and met him. He saw that she knew and he said nothing, got off the horse, and started walking back to town, with Tonsun walking beside him, silent.

Once as they walked he had looked at her and had seen tears down her cheeks, but she remained quiet. At Hensley's, she had entered first and seen the form on the table but did not look at it inside the sheet. She reached out and placed her hand on the sheet where the shoulder pushed out. Just a touch, then she had sobbed once, deeply, and said: "I go make box now. For ground I make box . . ."

The funeral had been strange. They hurried to get Wangsu in the ground because of the condition of the body. Tonsun had brought some small brass pots in which she burned incense with colored smoke, and all of the children were there—three boys and two girls —dressed and standing next to the grave in a neat row. Murphy was there, and Midge and Doc, and to Murphy's complete surprise, so was half the town. It seemed as if all the merchants and crib girls were old friends of Wangsu, even Tilman from the harness shop.

Tonsun had sung a kind of song, in Chinese, that moved in a series of lowering notes and finally ended in a mournful nasal hum. The song projected into the air a sadness that lasted, a palpable grief you could almost cut. Then they had lowered Wangsu into the ground in a raw pine box with a Chinese figure painted on the lid that Tonsun told him meant Good Journey or Happy Journey—and it was over.

Except that it wasn't. It was just starting. When the grave was covered, the store owner, the saloon keeper, Tilman and Wayne from the livery all came up to Tonsun and leaned down to whisper in her ear. She nodded to them, gave them small smiles, and they moved on. Murphy was close to her but could not hear the words; he decided it was none of his business but then changed his mind. There had been a killing; anything about it was his business. So he made their comments his business and decided he would ask Tonsun later.

But again he was a jump behind. When the burial was over and he was standing with Midge and Doc—

getting ready to walk from the dusty little graveyard east of town on the flats, the only place where the rocks were thin enough to allow graves to be dug— Tonsun had approached him.

She looked at Murphy, then the others, clearly uncomfortable about Midge and Doc. Finally she said to Murphy, "You come for tea?"

Murphy nodded. "We'd be glad to . . ."

"No, no." Tonsun was clearly perplexed now. Apparently, courtesy was such a part of her that she didn't know how to put it. She looked at Midge and Doc, waited, and Midge could see what she meant.

"I think she just wants you," Midge said to Murphy. "Not us . . ."

Tonsun shook her head and said to Midge and Doc, "You too, you both come to tea anytime, but later. Later. First must talk law."

And now Murphy sat, waiting to "talk law" at the low table again, smelling the tea. A different tea this time. Something thick and heavy that filled the air, or perhaps that was still the incense smell he'd noticed at the graveside. He was alone: Tonsun had gone to fetch something. After the ceremony he had gone back to his office and gotten his gun, which he'd taken off for the funeral, and walked to Wangsu's. She had shown him into the small room—in silence—where little Wong Ny had brought the tea settings. Then Tonsun had gone to get something, leaving him sitting.

He did not mind because it gave him time to formulate the questions he wanted to ask Tonsun. The answer to all this was somewhere in what people

91

weren't telling him, was somewhere in the small lies, the unanswered questions.

Tonsun càme into the room from outdoors and sat silently across the table. She had a small package wrapped in old sacking that she put on the table next to the pot. She then poured tea. Her eyes were red at the corners but there was no other indication of her sadness. Her back was straight and her hands steady as she poured. Murphy left the tea sitting, his hands still on his legs, palms flat.

"I'm sorry, Tonsun, but I have to ask you some questions."

She shook her head. "Not now. First must talk of job."

"Job?" He stared at her. "What job?"

She frowned. "Wangsu hire you now . . ."

"Wangsu? But he's dead . . . I mean . . ."

She nodded, looking up at him. "He dead. I understand. But Wangsu spirit still be—the spirit hire you. Wangsu honor hire you—all the same, Wangsu hire you."

"Hire me to do what?"

Now her eyes glittered with a bright hate, a shining hate. "Wangsu hire you to find man who . . . man who kill him. Wangsu hire for death. You find him and kill him. Wangsu pay."

Murphy shook his head. "No, Tonsun—no pay. You can't hire me to kill a man."

She held up her hands, nodded with great emphasis. "Can do, can do—have money. Have much money. Can pay, will pay for death. Will pay much money for death." She picked up the package and opened it, handed it to Murphy with the wrapping open, and he saw that it contained a small ingot of pure gold. He guessed five pounds.

"What in God's name . . . ? Where did you get this? Tonsun, this is solid gold."

She started crying now, her shoulders heaving. She leaned forward, sobbing. "Will pay much money for death."

Murphy reached across the table, took her hands. "Tonsun, listen, you can't pay me to kill someone. Even someone like the man who did this to Wangsu. That's not how the law works." He looked at the bar of gold again, gleaming in the light through the open door. "Not even for pure gold. I'll find the man who did this but you won't have to pay."

She nodded. "All the same, die for Wangsu? You find and kill for Wangsu?"

"No, no. I'll find him and bring him in and he'll hang—all the same. He'll die. You don't have to pay for it. The law works for nothing."

He released her hands, saw the gold again, nestling on the paper in the middle of the table. Could not keep his eyes from seeing the gold, as he said to her, "But I've got to ask you some questions—can you answer them for me?"

She was settled now, had what she wanted. She nodded.

Murphy took a breath, let it out. "Where did you get the gold?"

She didn't answer him, took a stubborn line to her jaw.

He decided to drop that question but asked another: "Why did you lie to me?"

She stared at him. "Lie?"

Murphy held his tea cup, dwarfing it. "You told me Wangsu was going to mail a package, but others told me they saw him headed west with a burro. And when . . . I found him he was with the burro. Where was he going, Tonsun? Where was he really going?"

She hesitated only for a second, then shook her head. "Don't know."

Murphy leaned back, sighed. "Tonsun, you have to help me—I can't find the man who did this unless you help me."

She looked frustrated. "All the same true—Tonsun no know. Wangsu take burro and go once, sometimes three times a month. Go for three days, four days. Come home." She shrugged. "Not know where. Only know what—go to work mine."

Murphy stared at her. "Mine? What mine? Is that where the gold came from?"

She looked startled. "Not mean to say. Not supposed to say mine."

"What mine?" Murphy pushed. "Did Wangsu have a mine near here?" For a time it didn't seem that she was going to answer. She looked away, out the open doorway. The light coming in framed her face with a harshness. He could see lines now around her eyes, could see some of her age. She was thinking, pulling at something, and he thought of how she would live now, with Wangsu gone and the children—wondered how they would get by.

At length she looked back at him, studied his face for another long time, until he felt she was looking not at him but inside him. Then she nodded. "Will tell."

He waited. Knowing when to back off was half of getting answers out of people.

"Wangsu . . . not . . . known."

Murphy didn't understand. "You mean by me? He wasn't known by me?"

She sipped tea. A delicate motion with a delicate cup and delicate hands. Then she put the cup down, studied him again. "By anybody. Wangsu not known by anybody."

"How do you mean?"

For a second a bitter look came into her eyes. "All the same everybody think Wangsu little Chinaman coming around to get laundry, sell food, clean up. All the same everybody think that's all Wangsu can be—call him little Chinaman." She hissed air through her teeth. "Wangsu more—Wangsu all."

Murphy remembered Wangsu working miracles on barren land with a hardwood stave and nodded. "I know what you mean . . ."

"No. Nobody know. All the same Wangsu coming for laundry and selling food, Wangsu watching town. Knowing town. Wangsu give money to town."

Murphy nodded. "I know—you told me that. He had to pay the town taxes and I think that was wrong . . ."

Tonsun shook her head. "No. More. Not just pay town for all the same law. Give money for new town. Give money for store. Give money for saloon. Give money for harness store."

Now he stared at her. "You mean he gave Tilman money? Gave them all money to rebuild?"

She nodded. "When you fight killer banker and town burn, no money in town because bank burn. Wangsu loan money to all of them."

God, Murphy thought. All this time and he hadn't

known. A whole substructure supporting the town and he hadn't known about it. A world within a world.

"Wangsu rich. Wangsu very rich, very honorable. Send gold back to family in Middle Country—you call China—every month. Many venerables live on Wangsu money. Many children live on Wangsu money. Every month Wangsu send gold back to San Francisco and back to family."

"All from a mine? From a mine around here?"

Now she shook her head. "Wangsu never say where. Just go with burro, come back with gold. Not say more."

"He didn't even tell you?"

Another shake. "It . . . not good. Not good to tell too much for China person. Better to all the same keep tongue. Saying in Middle Country: Crow who waggle tongue lose it. Wangsu not want family to know because they might say where. Not mean to but say anyway. Children talk, I talk. Better to keep tongue."

Murphy was stunned. All this time, Wangsu and Tonsun working in the garden, all this time Wangsu had a hidden mine. Not just a mine, but a paying mine—from the way it sounded, a big strike—in an area where hundreds, thousands of men had tried and missed. Incredible. "Did he ever say anything *about* the mine? Not where it was, but what kind of rock was there, anything?"

Tonsun thought, shook her head. "No. Just come home with gold, then go to get laundry or sell food. Never talk of mine. Even when alone." She pointed at the ingot on the table. "Take. Wangsu wish to pay, his honor wish to pay for death."

But Murphy stood now, leaving the ingot on the

table. "I told you how it works. You don't pay for the law. Especially you—after Wangsu rebuilt the town."

"All the same, man die?"

He didn't say anything, turned to leave, but he was thinking, the phrase rolling in his mind: all the same, the man die.

CHAPTER 10

THERE WAS STILL the town.

He knew what he had to do. He had to ride west, he had to go back into the Huerfano and he had to go in hard. Somewhere in the canyons he would find the answers to the questions; he would find the men who had tried to kill him, would perhaps find the man or men who killed Wangsu.

But there was still the town. And he was still responsible for peace and good order: That was why he was being paid. It was late afternoon and he hadn't made the rounds in four days. That wasn't good. Troublemakers could smell it, could smell the weakness; the drinkers in the saloon—the bar roosters who thought they were something and tried to use whiskey-nerve to prove it—needed to be held down every night.

When he was laid up at Doc's they had several days to get bad, really bad. There was still the town, and before Murphy left he had to make the town ready and make himself ready. He had to check the pulse of the town.

He went to Doc Hensley's, where he found Doc in back pouring some chemical from a large supply bottle into a smaller prescription bottle.

"How is she?" Doc asked. "Is she taking it all right?"

Murphy nodded. "I'd say so. Tell me, Doc, did you borrow money from Wangsu?"

Doc shook his head. "No, why?"

"Because if you didn't, you're about the only one in town who didn't. . . ." He took ten minutes and told Doc the whole story, covering everything.

Doc listened silently, at the end asking only one question. "Did she know where the mine was?"

Murphy shook his head. "Nothing about it."

Doc rubbed his hair back. "I don't understand how this could have been going on and we didn't know about it. Not a word."

Murphy agreed, but said nothing. Doc went back to work, then stopped and looked at Murphy. "What are you doing here?"

Blunt, Murphy thought, he's always been blunt—it's how he keeps from having nightmares, keeps honest. "I'm going back into the Huerfano."

"When?"

"Tomorrow morning."

It came without any hesitation. "You want me to ride with you?"

"No . . ."

"You think anybody else will go with you? Do you think Tilman or Wayne will ride into there with you?"

Murphy shook his head. "No. I don't expect them to—the same as I don't expect you to come with me. It's my job."

Doc set the full small bottles on a shelf, closed the big bottle, and put it away under the white chest in the corner. "Then why are you telling me?"

Murphy ran a hand over his face. "Two reasons. One, look at my side and retape it so if things get a little rough, I might have a chance. Two, Midge . . ."

Doc looked at him, waiting. "So? Midge, what?"

"Well, if something happens out in the canyons and I don't make it back—I had plenty of time to think about it when I started walking back after they shot the gray out from under me. If something happens and I don't make it, I want you to make sure Midge is, well, covered."

Doc nodded but gave a small laugh. "From what I've seen, it could work the other way—she'd wind up taking care of us, not us her."

"Just the same," Murphy said (realizing that he'd almost said "all the same"), "I'd feel better."

"It's done."

Murphy climbed up on the table and Doc pulled the bandage. "Looks good, looks good." He unrolled new gauze and covered the wound, taped it again, once more using several rolls of wide adhesive to bind the upper arm in place to keep it from moving. "If you could wait a few days . . ."

Murphy shook his head. "It's been too long already. Things like this have to be settled as soon as possible."

"I thought you'd say that." Doc finished and Murphy put his shirt back on, stood and jammed his hat down, walked out into the sun.

He cataloged the things he had to do: Make his day rounds, get ready, talk to Midge, then his night rounds. As he walked, he recalled a strange time when a man had come to Cincherville to kill him. Two mines had been stolen eight or ten years earlier and Murphy had found the man who had stolen the claims. The man had registered them in his own name. Murphy knew this but could not prove it.

Still, the man had been afraid, and he had hired another man to come to Cincherville and kill Murphy. Just garbage, Murphy remembered, the man was just garbage—somebody who shot from the night, lived in the night and, finally, died in the night when Murphy saw him in an alley ready to shoot and got three rounds out of the Smith first.

But before that night it had been tight for Murphy, knowing the man was coming to kill him but not knowing what the man looked like or when he would strike. A strange tight time, those nights, and to throw the man off—Murphy never did learn the man's name—he had changed the patterns of his rounds, sometimes not doing them at all.

He could not believe how it affected his life—just that, changing his rounds. So much of being a lawman was routine, and most of what counted people never saw. Making the rounds had been so regular, had been so much of his life, that when he changed it for that time it nearly made him stutter. It also turned the town upside down.

Making the rounds was important not for the act itself, but for what it meant—that order was being maintained, that somebody cared that things were kept moving in the right way. A man who would fight, who would cause trouble, might stop the wrong thinking simply because he saw a lawman making the rounds. There was no way to know how much trouble had been averted just because Murphy stopped by once in a while, pulled a doorknob at night, checked out an alley. It was, really, what law was all about. Making the rounds.

And when he didn't do it, or changed the order of it, he could feel the temper of the town change. That's how it was now. In the hotel, there was strain. Nothing to say, nothing to note, but a feeling, a curtness in everyone's manner. He went from the hotel to the dry goods, back to the harness shop—nodding, not talking of the attack or what he knew of Wangsu and the money many of them had borrowed. The feeling was everywhere, the strain, and it was when he was finished, when he was walking back across the street heading toward Midge's café, that he made the decision.

He was done with this town. When he had settled all this, when he came back from the Huerfano, he would go get Midge and they would leave. Even though they had nothing, they would leave. If they had to eat bugs, they would leave and take the rest of what they had coming and be happy. Find their niche. He knew he could not stay lucky forever, could not ride his luck much longer. They would get him. Maybe now, maybe in the canyons they would get him—but if not, if his luck held, he would come back and get Midge and they would leave, even if they had to walk. He would tell Midge tonight, after his night rounds.

He had coffee and a small lunch in the café but it was crowded and he didn't get time to say anything to Midge. After he'd eaten he went back to the office to catch up.

Ronnie Cline from the post office down in Greeley had sent all his mail up with the stage, and they had left it on Murphy's desk. Circulars, some wanted posters and notices, more advertisements for new "modern police equipment" with pictures of mustached Eastern policemen holding up new clubs or handcuffs or saps. He threw most of the papers in the stove, filed some letters in the desk drawer—they would have to be for whomever the town found next—and prepared himself for the Huerfano.

Weapons first. He had gone there once without thinking, undergunned and underplanned, and he would not do it again. He took down the double twelve Greener and broke it apart, stripped it down to the screws, and, with a small brush, cleaned every part. He checked all the springs, found a couple of spots of rust that he wiped oil into, then put it back together carefully. When he was done he dry-fired it several times on both hammers—not good for the gun, but this was the only way to check the action. He wrapped it in a clean cloth and then went to the ammunition. He found a box of double-ought buck in the desk drawer and set it on the desk. It would have been better to have new, but they didn't have double-ought at the store; whenever they did get some, there was no way of telling how long it had sat on some shelf in a warehouse.

He checked every shell—twenty of them. They were well waxed and all loaded with nine balls each, but they were black-powder shells, and black powder had a way of absorbing moisture and caking up. He held each shell next to his ear and shook it, setting aside any that didn't rustle. In the end he found he had only fourteen that he was certain of.

Only fourteen, he thought, smiling grimly. Hell, two would cut a horse in half—fourteen could clean out a town. I must be getting skittish in my old age. He suddenly remembered lying in back of the gray and hearing the slugs hitting the dead horse again, wished he had a hundred shells for the Greener.

After he had the shotgun ready he took a rifle from the rack over the chair and did the same, took it completely apart, oiled and brushed every screw and spring, and put it back together. Again he dry-fired it, and this time he was not satisfied; he found some small grating on the trigger let-off, so he took it apart again. There was a roughness on the end of the trigger sear and he used a sharpening stone to take it down, then reassembled the rifle once more and tried it, nodding when it dropped the hammer smoothly. The rifle was the same .45-70 he had carried when he went looking for Wangsu, and he found that four of the shells he had been carrying had caked powder and didn't rustle when shaken. He opened a new box of twenty, found them all to be good, and juggled boxes and shells until he had a box and a half—thirty rounds—which he put in a small cloth sack, leaving the rifle bare (it would go in the scabbard; the shotgun would be tied across the back of the cantle).

Then the Smith. It was coming on to evening now

but he didn't hurry the work. Again he disassembled the gun, cleaned it thoroughly, and put a light coat of oil on each piece as he put it back together, dry-firing when finished, checking to see that the cylinder rotated freely. He had gone to the new smokeless powder in his Smith loads—.44 Specials—and that kept the powder residue from clabbering up the cylinder and stopping it, but he checked it carefully anyway just as he checked the loads, shaking each one, though smokeless didn't take moisture like black powder.

There were no chances if a load misfired. If he found himself in a position where he had to shoot, he'd have to fire as fast and as accurately as he could, and he'd have no chance if his gun didn't work. Sometimes there was no chance even when it worked right. If a load didn't fire when he needed it, he might as well kiss life good-bye.

Most of being a lawman, Murphy thought, letting his mind freewheel while he worked, *most of all of it was checking doors.* He tried not to think of the other part, the times when he had to pop a cap and shoot. It came to that or it didn't, but he saw no point in thinking about it, just as it was pointless to think much about dying. Thinking of it did no good. It came or it didn't.

But riding into the Huerfano was different. There were men there who had tried to kill him once and he was certain they would try again. This time he had to think of it, prepare himself mentally and physically for it.

When the weapons were completed he went back over to his room at the hotel. He would have liked a bath—always go in clean, an old sergeant in the army had told him once, because it reduces the risk of infection if you get hit. "Go in clean and empty," the sergeant had rumbled to the recruits, "and you won't have so much to clean out of your pants." Coming from an old sergeant who smelled like he hadn't bathed since he was a sprout, it was strange advice.

Murphy wished he could take a bath now but the wound kept him from sitting in water. Instead he got hot water from the bathing shed in back, took it to his room, and did a cloth bath. Afterward he changed everything, clean underwear and up, shaved carefully by the light of the oil lamp on the wall—it was getting dim outside and the rooms at the rear of the hotel didn't get much daylight at the best of times. Then he rebuckled his gun belt and went out.

His plan was simple. He would eat lightly and give the saloon time to cook up, then he would make his night rounds and bed the town down. He'd ride out in the first part of morning, one or two o'clock. That would get him into the canyons just at daylight, with the sun coming up in back of him and everybody asleep.

A simple plan.

Except that things never seemed to go quite as planned.

CHAPTER 11

IT WASN'T THAT things had gotten bad, so much as they'd gotten wild. Coupled with Murphy's time away from his rounds, the word had gotten out that there was a strike.

It always amazed Murphy when news about a strike began to spread. Most of the time it was wrong. Men worked so hard they died, literally died with a pick in their hands, and found nothing; worked all that they were into the ground and found less than if they had stayed in Iowa and tended sheep. And perhaps because of the work, the crippling dirty work, let one man find so much as a smell of color and it became Golconda—a bonanza, the Comstock—the greatest motherlode in history.

Madness. Like water—no, like fire it spread, faster somehow than it seemed possible to spread. A strike! The news roared through the towns and camps, up and down the mountains into every corner and toilet and saloon and whorehouse; under every rock it was known instantly and the rush was on. Murphy had seen it ten, twelve times, always wrong, and it was like kicking the top off an anthill. Spreading madness.

Men came from everywhere—walking, running, riding, dragging—and with the prospectors, the dreamers, came those who made the only true money, the bloodsuckers—crib girls, gamblers, con men and hugger-muggers, hustlers, silver-tongued preachers who sold God for coin and gave nothing in return. The slicks who greased and took and won, as well as the robbers who just took with force, came to prey on the prospectors.

The first stages had hit Cincherville. The mad rush hadn't come yet but would, in days. Now there was just the word. *A strike, a strike so rich the vein carried the sun into the center of the earth; not silver, not such a low thing. Gold, the yellow beauty. Gold, to shine forever, and they had hit it big—as big as you could hit it, by God—had found a mountain of gold without even trying.*

Murphy came out of his room to a changed world. The hotel was starting to hum, had a new life, a sudden activity that hadn't been there a few hours before. In the street there were men pacing with a new speed, a new purpose, and he went to Midge's to find a crowd.

Midge looked harried, carrying bowls of stew to men who didn't care any longer what it cost. Just in that way everything had changed, in moments it had changed. Cincherville was no longer a dead town, it was crawling up, teeming with life. Human ants. Murphy nodded to Midge, smiled, and decided against eating. He had taken a big meal earlier and it would be better not to fill his stomach. He had wanted to speak to her of his decision to leave but he knew that could wait until he got back. If he got back. If he didn't get back, his decision didn't matter.

The saloon was pandemonium. It was still a shed of gray and raw wood, with a plank bar and some coarse tables in the back covered with blankets for cards, but the place had changed. The air was charged, like powder ready to blow, and it was filled with men: swearing, drinking, hell-raising, spitting on the floor, pushing each other, stinking, slamming shots back, gambling money they didn't have yet and would never see, getting disease from and giving disease to the crib girls, puking on the back wall to make room for more and more and more. . . .

Murphy stepped into the muck, into the stink and smoke of the room, and moved to the side of the door. He knew some of them and respected them, knew others and wished he didn't, but most of them he didn't know at all. The saloon owner was a greasy little man named Nickerson, and he held up a bottle and a glass with a question in his eyes when he saw Murphy.

Murphy shook his head. The bar whiskey would lift paint, was little more than straight grain alcohol mixed with a little coffee for color, and Murphy liked his blended, if at all—he had nearly stopped drinking.

He stood for a time and watched the room. Some men looked at him in open curiosity—had heard about the shooting—and others took the quick glance that meant some kind of guilt, but he let it go. He was looking for potential troublemakers. He did not want to stay long, just wanted to settle things down. It took him only half a minute to find what he was after.

There was a big man at the corner of the bar. He had looked at Murphy with an open challenge in his eyes—the rooster look. It would come from there and would come soon.

Murphy went to the bar. "What the hell's going on?"

Nickerson stopped in front of him. "You haven't heard? There's a strike up in one of the side canyons off the Huerfano. Big strike. They say it's the biggest they've ever seen."

"They always say it's the biggest they've ever seen. Who made it?"

Nickerson shrugged. "I don't know them. Some new mining company from San Francisco, come in with a new kind of machinery or something. Hit it right off the bat in that first canyon to the right when you go into the Huerfano. God, the luck."

Young, Murphy thought. Arvis Young comes in and spreads a little bull and hits gold. Or maybe not. Something prodded his thinking but he couldn't pin it down. Some small thing. "Any of them in here drinking?"

Nickerson shook his head. "Naw, these are all boogers looking to get rich. The real ones are up there digging it out—they'll come in later, though; you know how it works. They'll have to spend it sooner or later. . . ."

It came then. Murphy felt the slap on his shoulder and turned. The man who had looked at him with the rooster look was standing there. It's coming to me, Murphy thought—something about the mine. No, something about Young and the mine. Tickling around the edges. He looked at the man in front of him. Tall, taller than Murphy and bigger. Thick hair—nostrils and ears full of it. Thick neck; knife scar on his chin; round shoulders; strong build, but his legs not set right, back on his heels, half off balance.

"I hear you think you're the top dog around here," he said to Murphy.

The voice was arrogant, tough, easy-cheap. He was a bully when he was a kid, Murphy thought, always looking to prove how tough he was by picking on smaller kids. His breath smelled of rotten teeth and bar whiskey. Breath like puke.

Murphy hit him solidly. Holding his left arm still to protect the wound, he brought his right fist up from the bottom and hit the man in the diaphragm, aiming for a point somewhere to the rear of his back, putting all his weight behind the blow, hit him so hard the snot flew out of his nose and the man's eyes rolled white with the pain.

Then another hit, in the same place, and as the man leaned over, whistling air through his nose, beginning to vomit, Murphy hit him again, behind the ear, and the man went down like a shot steer.

"I don't want any trouble," Nickerson said. The whole thing hadn't taken three seconds. "No trouble at all . . ."

"You won't have any now. When he comes around

give him a beer and sit him in a chair. He'll be sore for a day or two but he'll be gentle."

Murphy looked around the room. The noise had stopped and everybody was staring at him. Somebody said once that nothing draws like a dogfight, Murphy thought, but they were wrong. It's men fighting that pulls attention. Get a couple of rummies going at each other and the world stops to watch. But now they knew, the law was back on the street. He said nothing, turned and walked out, but the noise had started again before he hit the door.

Outside it was dark but still a bit early to start for the Huerfano—he wanted to start in with the light at his back. Across the street there were still yellow lights coming from Midge's as she cleaned and got ready to close up for the night and go to her room. He thought deeply of going to her. Now. Just go into the cheery yellow light from the windows and to hell with everything else. His legs started taking him in that direction, and he thought of spending the night with her, of the soft light on her. Then he thought of what waited in the Huerfano for him, of the hard things there. It was tough for him, took all of him not to go to her.

But there was Wangsu, and the way Tonsun had crumpled inside herself when she saw Murphy riding up the day he found the body. There was Wangsu, and the cuts—the way they had used a knife on him . . . that was it. That was the thing in his memory. Something about a knife.

The men shooting at him in the canyon. One of them had said something about what their boss had done with a knife. Wangsu had been tortured with a knife.

Threads. Threads that held the questions together. That's what he was looking for now. Small threads to pull it together.

Wangsu was killed with a knife or knives. . . .

The men in the canyon talked of knives. . . .

Wangsu had a mine with gold, a good strike. . . .

A new strike had suddenly been made just after Wangsu had been tortured to death. . . .

By Arvis Young, who had hard eyes.

Murphy was stopped now in the middle of the street, standing to the dark side, his mind suddenly tumbling with the thoughts. There it was—maybe not all right but carrying something close to right.

Arvis Young, who had hard eyes, also had a new strike and Wangsu had been killed for a gold mine, for a rich gold mine. Somebody had tortured him to find the location? Yeah, that worked. Then they had claimed the mine that Wangsu had never claimed, had kept secret because he had been worried—just as Tonsun still worried—that because he was Chinese, the law would not be *all the same* as it was for whites.

But how could Young come into town and find out something not a soul, including Murphy, had known? Even Tonsun knew only there was a mine, not where it was; how could a stranger come into town and inside of a few days not only know there was gold, but know who had it and how to find it? It was impossible for him to have come to Cincherville and have found out in such a short time. He must have known before he came.

From San Francisco.

Ahh, the last piece. Murphy felt the muscles in his jaw tighten. That made it fit. Young had come from San Francisco; every month, rain or shine, Wangsu had shipped gold to the broker in San Francisco for reshipment to his family in China.

Murphy walked now toward the livery. Pushing midnight, still a little early, but he wasn't going to wait any longer. He could smell it now, he would take it now, take the scent and run with it because of what he was; until he left with Midge that's still what he was—the law.

Young had come into his town, his country, and killed. There had been a leak in San Francisco, and Young had found out about the gold. He had come knowing there was gold, knowing who had it, knowing it was Wangsu. Then he had laid for him, taken him to the old shack and carved him up until Wangsu gave out the location of the mine.

It all worked.

And when Murphy had started to ride out to the Huerfano the first time Young must have thought Murphy was onto something and decided to take care of him then, set the ambush up. Three men with all the bullets in the world. He must have brought a whole crew of toughs in with him from San Francisco. All along he was thinking ahead of Murphy, knew there was gold in Murphy's town when Murphy didn't know, knew Murphy was riding west and when, knew that Murphy would be the thorn in his paw, knew that he had to take Murphy out. Young knew it all, had set it all up.

There was just one variable he hadn't counted on. Murphy had dropped his hat, and the bullets that would have killed him went high.

Now that Murphy knew who was behind this mess, he wasn't about to ride into another ambush.

CHAPTER 12

THE BAY DIDN'T want to get up. Murphy had heard that old saw about horses sleeping standing up and knew that they did, or dozed that way. But they also slept flat on their sides—he knew an old buckskin cow pony that slept on his stomach like a farm dog. When he found the bay in back of the livery in the corral it was down, its eyes shut, and snoring with a rumble that puffed dirt in front of its nose with each breath.

Murphy had to drag it to its feet using the halter, and saddle it while almost holding it up. The bay yawned and stretched and belched and farted and kept trying to go back to sleep and didn't come fully awake until Murphy had led it back across the street to the office to get the Greener and the rifle.

The lights were out in Midge's but he knew she

would be lying awake for a while, waiting to see if he would come. Sometimes he did, letting himself in the back way, and there was that gentleness between them and he would let himself out before dawn. It was silly, because neither of them really gave a damn what anybody thought, but they still did it. Part of him wanted to be there with Midge, but he knew if he went in, he would stay, and there was this thing to clean up with Young and the Wangsu mine. He already thought of it as Wangsu's mine.

He rode by her door, let the bay set its own pace—a half-asleep walk—since he was leaving early, and threaded his way through the houses on the west side of town.

There were no lights in the windows. And when he looked back on the town spread out below him, he could see the only building with lights in the windows was the saloon. They would be done soon, he knew—even the hard-edge drinkers who drank to die each night could only hold so much, and they passed out, especially on bar whiskey. Lucky not to go blind on it. And the town would sleep—or not sleep so much as stop—for the few hours until daylight.

The bay was slowing—probably starting to doze—and he heeled it lightly. He did not wear spurs because they made noise and sometimes made it hard to move fast, but he missed them now and then, missed the little squirt they gave a horse.

The bay picked up and started to pay attention to the trail. It was pitch dark, as if the sky had been painted with black paint, even the light from the stars absorbed by cloudy blackness. When his eyes became accustomed to the darkness he could see the horse's ears slightly, and the back of the mane, but no farther. The trail was gone to him and he had to trust the horse's judgment and would have worried, except that the bay was fully awake now and seemed to know what it was doing.

He rode a mile walking, then another, and could still see nothing. He thought of stopping to wait for better light but decided to wait until he was closer, then he'd pull off to the side and time his getting into the Huerfano so the sunrise would be working with him.

This was like riding in a sack, he thought. Sitting on the horse moving forward in a sack tied up so he couldn't see anything. Seven miles out, the horse perked its ears and stopped; Murphy was about to heel it forward again when he heard it.

Hooves coming toward him at a slow trot. He pulled the bay over to the side, in back of some small boulders, and waited. In moments three shadows, horses and men, cut against the dark and trotted by. They said nothing, passed not fifteen feet from where Murphy sat on the bay, watching, but had no idea he was there. Murphy was glad his horse didn't snort or whinny at the other horses. The men were riding with a purpose, said nothing, and that threw Murphy off.

It was strange to be riding into Cincherville with such purpose at three, four in the morning. It was not a time to ride for good reasons, and he thought of following them, checking on them—Lord knows he could ride right on them and they wouldn't know he was there. Then it struck him that Young might be sending more men in to kill him, to finish the job they had started in the ambush, in which event it would be just as well to let them go, while he headed up into the canyons. They wouldn't find him in town and at least that would be three men he didn't have to face when he came against Young.

So he let them go, and when they were far enough off, he pulled the bay onto the trail again and started riding. He wasn't sure how far he'd come until he came into the basin. The body of the gray was nearly gone—the coyotes and buzzards had been there, as well as the flies—but the smell was high and his new bay went through like it was walking on eggs.

He was three miles from the first side canyons, where he guessed the mine would be. Perhaps four miles. He raised in the saddle and looked back to the east. Just a line of gray—if he looked directly at it he couldn't see it—was cutting across the horizon out in the flats, and he realized the bay was moving more slowly than he had thought. Dawn would be coming and he wouldn't have to wait.

He visualized the Huerfano canyons and the way they laid. It was like a hand, held flat down, the wrist being the entry to the main canyon, which ran back and would be the middle, or longest, finger. The side canyons went off this main trunk like the fingers of the hand.

Murphy entered the wrist area just at dawn. The main canyon was where the shacks formed what could be called a settlement, but he had decided to start with the first canyon to the right, based on what the saloon owner had said, and he rode into the canyon mouth carefully. It was not a good place to be: narrow, an old streambed that might run in the spring if it was a heavy snow year. He had to take the bay through a rock-walled notch so narrow he could nearly touch both sides. The horse's hooves echoed against the rock walls and the noise carried out ahead of him. He had left the Greener across the cantle while riding in the dark but he untied it now, took it out of the wrapping and loaded it. There might not be time for the Smith. With the hammers at half cock, he nudged the bay into a faster walk and he rode into the canyon taking small half breaths, ready to cut down with the Greener at the slightest movement.

It never came.

A quarter of a mile into the canyon the stream widened. He took a deep breath and pulled the bay to the side, hating to ride in the middle when coming into trouble, liking to be close to cover, and stopped under a slight overhang. Ahead he could see the canyon walls, rising like fluted columns, rock cliffs catching the new morning sun and flashing red-gold.

As he sat looking, easing his weight in the saddle, he heard sounds ahead—sounds of a mining camp waking up. There was the clatter of metal, men swearing and yelling, doors slamming. He was close, just around the corner, and he swung off the horse to walk. Once during an attack he had missed his target because his horse had moved under him. Murphy had taken a bullet in the leg, and he had never made that mistake again.

With the reins in his hand, the bay following, the shotgun and handgun in both hands and ready, his fingers on the triggers, he tucked himself in back of a rock edge and looked around the corner and into the camp.

CHAPTER 13

BEFORE HE STUCK his head out, he removed his hat and then took one quick look into the camp at what lay before him. Straight ahead, the canyon opened into a basin not unlike where they had shot the gray out from under him. In the middle of the basin were three new buildings. They were made of old lumber taken from other mines and shacks in the canyons, but the boards had new-sawn edges. A bunkhouse was to the right, long and low with a shed roof and a rough rack in front with a washstand. Directly in the middle stood a work shed, closed on three sides and open on the front, full of tools, mining equipment, and harnesses.

To the left of the work shed was a small hut that must have been the mine headquarters. Above all three buildings, on the side of the canyon, was a mine opening that looked like the mouth to a small cave.

There was only a short pile of tailings in front of the mine entry—either it was truly a good strike or they were just starting to dig—with no set of tracks for a rail dump car to bring the ore out. All of this Murphy saw in two seconds, letting his eyes sweep over and gather everything in, filling his mind with the picture in front of him.

This and one more thing: There were men everywhere. A quick count made twelve—two by the headquarters hut, five in the tool shed and five by the bunkhouse. There might be more inside the buildings or down in the mine; he couldn't be sure. He could see twelve and that was plenty.

He thought on the best plan. He could work back down the canyon and come up on the side, tie the bay somewhere, and take his time. But the cliffs were sheer and rocky; he would be bound to knock some gravel loose. They'd see him and nail him like a bug up on the side of a wall. When was it? Yeah, back in New York when he was a kid, big and raw and stupid—there was a cop who kept him out of trouble, not all of it but some. That cop had given him some advice about fighting. Something about how if you're going to fight, fight—get right into the middle of the biggest part and let go. Do the unexpected.

Murphy took a deep breath. Might as well jump in the middle. He brought the barrel of the shotgun up, not aimed at anybody but not too far off either, squared his hat, and walked around the curve of the rock, keeping slightly to the right, heading for the middle of the mining camp, which was forty, fifty yards away.

They didn't all see him at once. Two did, and

stopped, looking at him. Then another one, then three more and another one, until all of them had stopped what they were doing and had turned to face Murphy. One man at the washstand had soap and water on his face, and he grabbed a dirty towel hanging on a nail on the bunkhouse wall and wiped his eyes, then stood wiping his hands, watching Murphy come toward them.

He couldn't see Arvis Young or any of the four men he had jailed in Cincherville. He knew none of these men, had never seen them before, and was sure none of them had been in town. None of them seemed to be wearing a gun—it would have been impossible to work in a mine with a gun on—but two men in the toolshed were standing near a couple of rifles that leaned against the back corner. All strangers, they must have all come in from San Francisco with Young. But they knew him. They knew Murphy.

One man on the left side of the toolshed picked up a pick handle and held it ready in his right hand. Another man grabbed a shovel. Murphy stepped closer, swung the barrel of the Greener up until it covered the man with the pick handle. "I don't think you want any of this . . ." said Murphy. The man put the pick down but one man moved near the rifles. Murphy watched him, but other men started to move as well, out to the sides, and he couldn't watch them all well enough. If they were crazy enough to come for him, he thought, they would get him. He could get two with the shotgun, two more with the handgun, and they'd be on him. If they were crazy enough. He had to handle this and handle it fast.

124

"I'm looking for Young. Where is he?"

Nobody answered. A full minute passed, a minute that felt like a year. Then one man stepped forward two steps. Thirty yards, maybe twenty-five.

"Young isn't here. What do you want?"

"Where is he?"

"Gone. Him and two others rode out this morning. Early." He looked at the other men, got brave. "Listen, the word we got was nobody comes in. Nobody."

They rode by me, Murphy thought. The three of them rode by me heading for town. They were going in to kill me—why else would they be riding into town? If I stay here and make trouble, it won't do any good. I'll have to pull out of this and go for Young. Get him and I've got them all. Just like cutting the head off a snake.

"When he gets back, tell Young I want to see him."

The statement meant nothing, they knew he knew more, but it gave the situation a way down, a way for him to leave. This is working, he thought—they're going to let me leave. He started to back away, a short step at a time. Two steps more and he would be around the curve again, at his horse and gone.

One more step and it happened, came the way it always came. A small movement to the right, behind in the toolshed, a man who lowered his shoulder too fast in the back of the toolshed and came up with one of the rifles, cocking and firing it as he brought the barrel up—firing too soon, so that the bullet took the earth low and to the right of Murphy's foot. Murphy dropped the hammer on the Greener and blew the man nearly through the back of the toolshed.

For a second, a long second, there was nothing and it could have gone either way. The man had been hit solidly, did not move after he was down, and there was silence, silence that filled the morning and hummed. Murphy looked for a sign, a small sign of which way it would go, wishing he had about three more Greeners ready.

One of the men swore.

"Ahh, hell, I didn't sign on for all this . . ." The man at the bunkhouse threw the towel down.

"Shut up, Harris," the man who had held the pick handle said. "You signed just like we all did." He was obviously a foreman. Big shoulders, heavy arms, curved back, legs like tree trunks.

"Not for this. I signed for a bonus because there might be some rough stuff—maybe some knuckles with other miners. I didn't sign for trouble with the law. I'm a miner, and I've done some things I ain't proud of, but I ain't digging for no outfit that cuts no Chinese to pieces that way."

"Dammit, Harris, you don't know what you're talking about."

"You mean I know more than I'm supposed to know." Harris turned to Murphy and said, "I walked by the head shack in the middle of the night on my way to get rid of some beans and heard them talking. Was I you, lawman, I'd cut and ride back to town. They're fixing to take your woman."

Murphy's stomach tightened up into his throat. "What are you talking about?"

The foreman moved forward. "One more word, Harris, and you're done . . ."

"You talk again," Murphy said, swinging the Greener onto the foreman, "and they'll have to bury you in four places. Tell me, Harris. Now. What about my woman?" Midge, he thought. Not Midge. Keep Midge from this.

"I heard them talking last night, middle of the night. Young said he wanted you gone and that the other men had screwed it up. They figured you were too hard to take, and Young said he had a way, said he'd get your woman and take her and you'd come for her and they could get you that way. He said it was your only weak spot, the woman. That's where they were riding this morning, to get your woman and you. . . ."

Murphy held up a hand. "Harris, I'm leaving. I want everybody gone but you and another man you can trust. The two of you guard this mine until I get back. Can you handle that?"

Harris spit in the dirt at his feet and looked at the foreman. "I got no trouble with that."

Murphy turned and trotted around the corner to the bay. Whether Harris could handle it or not didn't matter; the mine didn't matter, the gold didn't matter, Wangsu, the law, his life, none of it mattered to Murphy right now.

Young, who had tortured and mutilated Wangsu to find the mine, was going to take Midge to draw Murphy into killing range.

Well by God, it worked, he thought, swinging a leg over the bay and tearing the horse's head around and down-canyon. He slammed his heels into the bay's ribs so hard the wind whistled out of its nostrils. You got what you wanted, Young. I'm coming for you and if you touch her, if you so much as touch her, you'll wish to God you'd never been born.

I'm coming, Young.

CHAPTER 14

HAD HIS MIND been on the horse, Murphy would have been surprised and amazed at the bay. Bad front shoulders or not, it gave all it had and didn't go down. He would have seen or felt the bay go through a wall and come out the other side a tough, experienced horse that knew what it could and could not do, and controlled itself to get all it could out of its body. A rare thing. Murphy drove it like a machine, drove it to where many horses would have gone down, would have died. The bay took it all, settled in and paced itself. The first time it faltered they were only a mile out of Cincherville and it had held a mile-eating lope all the way. It was frothed, sweaty, and covered with spit but it wasn't down; had Murphy been aware of the animal, he would have realized how good a horse he had in the bay.

Had he been aware of it. Aware of anything. Only

Midge filled his mind. Midge and a terrible worry, a sick worry that he had waited too long to say things, too long to do things, and now it was too late.

Midge and Young.

Cincherville came over the horse's ears and Murphy reined in. Some sense had to be there, he had to apply some sense to his actions. It wouldn't do any good for Midge if he allowed himself to be slaughtered like beef. He had to think right, do right. First, see if it's true. Check the café.

He pulled the bay up in front of the café. The door was open and there were no customers inside. The front was empty. In the kitchen, he felt the stove and found it cold. There was a bowl with three or four pounds of flour in it on the table in the middle of the kitchen. She had started to make biscuits when they came in. Early then, just at dawn while he was riding into the Huerfano they had come into the café and she had turned, with flour on her cheek like she always had, had turned when they came into the kitchen and brushed her hair back . . .

Stop it, he told himself.

They would have left some sign for him. They wanted him to follow, Young wanted him to tear after them—they would have left some sign. He looked around the kitchen, saw nothing, then went back into the front. It was under the sugar bowl at the front table. A note:

SAME PLACE AS CHINAMAN.

Of course. Murphy should have guessed. He crumpled the note and stepped outside. Noon, or close to it. People were starting to come to the café for lunch. Tilman from the harness shop always came over for stew and biscuits; he had closed his shop and started across.

I need a horse, Murphy thought. The bay was still all there but down and tired. To stick another nine on it would be asking too much. That horse wouldn't make it. Tilman came up to him.

"What's the matter with Midge? She wasn't there for breakfast and I don't smell any cooking now. . . ."

Murphy ignored him and untied the bay from the hitchrail, led it up to the livery. Wayne was there, forking some hay into the stalls.

"Give me a good horse. Now."

Wayne saw his eyes and nodded, saying nothing. He went to the corral in back and came back with a sorrel. Good size but thin in the legs. It didn't matter. Nothing mattered. Murphy pulled his saddle off the bay and threw the blanket and saddle over the sorrel in one motion. He jerked the cinch, let the horse blow air and tightened the cinch down. Everything he did was as automatic as breathing. Some people had gathered, people from the stores who had put two and two together and figured that Midge being gone and Murphy riding out were tied together. Some of them asked questions, pushed and prodded.

He didn't care. He didn't answer.

They'll kill her, he thought. They have to kill her because she knows now. Young will kill her but he'll wait until he has me.

"I'll grain the bay and rub it down . . . ," Wayne said but Murphy was on the sorrel and riding before he got the words out.

They'll have to kill her but they won't do it until they have me.

It was like a chant as he drove the sorrel up, into a hard gallop, then down into the ground-covering lope he needed.

He pointed the sorrel at the canyon where he'd found Wangsu's body.

Until they have me—that's how long she's got.

He had to get his thinking right. Worry over Midge had him frantic, clawing at hope the way a badger digs a hole, ripping and tearing at it. But that wouldn't help her. He had to put her away in his mind, stop thinking of her and think only of how to take Young and the two men.

The sorrel started to slow and Murphy slammed his heels into the horse, holding it in a high canter. They might not wait for him to get there to hit him—Young might set it up before then. They would know he was coming, where he was coming, and approximately when—Young might figure to catch him off guard and take him on the way in. Murphy had to think ahead of them now—if there was any chance for Midge, any chance at all, it would come only if he could think ahead of Young.

Catch them off guard. He thought of the trail ahead, tried to remember how it had looked riding up to the rim country. One place it narrowed, as it started up into the foothills leading to the rim. If they were going to try for him on the way in, that's where it would be. Where it narrowed and where he had to ride in a predictable line. How far from there to the shacks where he'd found Wangsu? A mile? No, less—half a mile.

He'd go off to the side there, work around in back of them. Get rid of the horse. He used the tail of the reins to whip the sorrel into more speed and covered the next four miles in just over twenty minutes. Ahead in the noon sun lay the point where the trail narrowed. He had been running in a draw that opened out, and before it opened, he pulled the sorrel up and swung down.

He pulled the rifle from the scabbard and untied the shotgun from in back of the cantle. It took him a moment to find the shells in the saddlebag and fill his pockets with extra loads for both guns. Then he tied the sorrel to some brush and faced the narrows and rim ahead. It was like a rear gun sight, the notch he would have had to ride through, with the two ears of the sight shale slopes that fed up into the rim edge. To work around, he would have to climb the slopes and move along the base of the rim, then work back down to the shacks in the old settlement area where Young was holding Midge— or said he was holding her. He stuck the cut-off shotgun through his belt and carried the rifle with a shell in the bore, the hammer on half cock. He set off at a shuffling run to the right. He had a mile and a half to go, a lot of it climbing, figure another half hour to the mine slope up in back of the shacks.

He ran a hundred yards, stopped and studied the terrain ahead; then another hundred, climbing through rocks and brush, stopping to scan again. He didn't see the man until he was at the top, near the rim edge and looking back and down. Then he caught movement, a twitch of cloth, and he dropped and watched where he'd seen the color move, holding his breath, hating the wait.

There, he saw it again, and then made out the shape of a man in back of a rock ledge, lying on his stomach beneath a stump of scraggly piñon. Too far to see who it was, but he was certain it wasn't Young, would be one of the miners. He brought the rifle up, settled the front sight on the man, and started to squeeze, but held it. If he popped now, they would know he was coming in the shacks. There were still two of them, Young and the other miner. He would go around this one.

He eased the hammer down on the rifle and took a breath. The shacks were still not in sight but he knew he was close, just around the edge of the shale and down. The man below was intently staring at the notch before him and Murphy lowered himself behind some broken rocks, square chunks that had broken off the rim and fallen. He worked silently across the top of the shale and out of sight of the sniper. Another hundred yards and he raised his head carefully over a broken slab of shale and saw the cabin below.

Three horses were tied in front, not far from the bones of the burro, and a man sat casually on the front steps of the shack in which Murphy had found Wangsu's body.

Two. It was close to a hundred and fifty yards but he could see that the man wasn't Young and he thought, Two, that's two of them. Using a rest, he could take the man from here with the .45-70, a long shot but he could do it. He eased the rifle onto the shale and steadied it with his hand. Midge must be in the shack and there was danger if he shot, but he could not get closer than this, and this was a chance to take one of them out. He supposed Young was inside. Maybe he'd come running out when Murphy fired and he could catch him with a second shot.

He held his aim on top of the man's head, figured to drop a good foot from here, eared the hammer back, took a full breath, let half of it out, and squeezed gently.

The recoil drove his shoulder back as the big slug belched out in a cloud of black smoke. The man sitting on the front steps was wiped back and down as if slapped by a giant hand.

Murphy levered another round in and waited, the hammer back, holding his breath. The heat cooked him, baked him in the silence after the rifle fire, but nobody came out of the shack. Half a minute passed and he knew he was going to have to do something— move, take the man on the left, whom he could now hear scrabbling up the shale slope, brought by the sound of the rifle. Murphy began to wheel in that direction when he heard the sound, in back of him, up the slope—he knew that it was Young behind him.

"Let the rifle lay and stand." The voice was steady, measured, not excited. It came from the slope in back of him, and Murphy thought, I wonder why he doesn't just shoot? Just pull the trigger and put one in me? He thought momentarily, insanely, that he might wheel and get a round off but knew Young would be ready for that.

Murphy lay the rifle down and stood.

"Now turn, slowly, and throw that shotgun and the handgun away. With one hand. Just the fingers."

Still he doesn't shoot, Murphy thought—why? He

pulled the shotgun out of his belt and dropped it and the Smith in the rocks.

I just killed one of his men and he won't pull the trigger? Something was there, some other thing that kept him from shooting.

"You caused me some trouble," Young said as Murphy turned. "I figured you'd come in high on us, so I waited. But I was over a little too far and didn't get to you in time to save Pooter."

"Where's Midge?"

Young nodded. "You would ask that first. She's in the shack, tied to a bunk. She was safe when I left her but I can't guarantee anything. Pooter was down there a long time alone with her and he always was one to take advantage of a situation . . ."

There was a quiet coldness in Murphy now. He was beyond anger, was in a place where only one thing mattered—to destroy the man in front of him. He knew now why Young hadn't shot him, could smell it and see it in him. He also knew that it could be his only advantage; Young had kept him alive for the same reason he had kept Wangsu alive as long as possible—he liked it. He wanted to get Murphy for having caused him difficulty, wanted to torture him, mentally and perhaps physically. It was the only reason Murphy still lived.

The other man came around the edge of the shale now, breathing hard, holding his rifle in front of him. "I heard the shot and, oh, you got him."

Young pointed to the shack with his chin and said to Murphy, "Start walking now. Ahead of us, down the slope."

Murphy eased down the slope. If he had a chance, there would only be one, and he didn't have a gun. He would need everything in his body, everything he had ever *been* to take them both with his hands.

Not now, not walking down the slope. They stayed well to the rear of him, both rifles aimed at his back. Even if one stumbled, the other one would have him. He had to wait, wait until he got to the shack.

At the bottom of the slope he slowed and stumbled a bit intentionally, looked back quickly to locate them accurately. Young was to the front about three paces, the other man slightly back and to the left of Young, holding his rifle loosely, almost relaxed.

Thirty paces to the shack. He could smell it now, the blood and rot-smell still there from Wangsu and the burro. Midge in there, he thought, tied in there, and Pooter in there with her, in that stink. He shut his mind to it, time for that later. Only at the shack would he have a chance, only then, before they could get rope on him.

The body of the man he had shot in the chest with the .45-70 was sprawled away from the door, and Murphy dismissed him, began to work on his move, when he caught a glint of metal in the dirt, just to the left of the door. It was the man's gun, knocked out of his holster when the big slug took him away from the step.

Oh, Murphy thought. Just that: Oh. Six steps, five—coming now, the time was coming. He would have to fall down and to the left, all in one motion, and get the gun and turn and fire. All in one smooth motion.

"Hold it." Young's voice cut his thinking. "Carlson —Pooter's gun is there in the dirt. Go kick it out of the way so our friend here doesn't get ideas."

Damn. One chance, and it was gone.

Carlson did as he was told, stepped around Murphy and kicked the handgun back under the shack and that put him in front of Murphy, to the left of the door. Two steps now to the door, one, it had to be now. It had to be now . . .

Murphy stepped up and started into the shack and saw Midge tied to an old bunk against the wall, registered it: her eyes big and red from crying, her dress ripped, her mouth open in an O. He took all of that in as he was moving. Half a step in through the doorway, his back and shoulders filled with a terrible tightness, his mind filled with a cold death rage, he turned and hit Carlson in the face with his right fist so hard that it jarred his elbow socket, set his shoulder on fire; only one blow, but he had given it all that he was, all that he could find for strength. He heard, felt Carlson's nose shatter and drive back and up, saw the whites of his eyes come, and knew that it was ended for him, that Carlson was gone.

Then down and around, grabbing the rifle out of Carlson's dying hands—knowing he was too late, that he would never wheel in time but moving, always moving, clawing the hammer back with his thumb and firing before he was around, firing before it was right to fire, firing because he had no time.

Young fired in the same moment, the slug cutting through Murphy's left arm just above the elbow. Simultaneously, Murphy's bullet traveled down the side of the barrel of Young's rifle, catching the edge of the forward hand guard and slamming Young's weapon back and down, out of his hands, sliding it away along the ground.

"Damn . . ." Young clawed for his handgun but his hand was numb. He got his hand on it, pulled it free of the holster, but his thumb couldn't work on the hammer and he fumbled.

Now it was there. Murphy knew nothing now, did not feel the wound in his left arm, did not think of Midge, knew only that it was there now, the chance, the time. He launched himself from the step, a sound in his throat, a ripping sound, and hit Young with his shoulder, drove the big man back and down, knocked the gun out of his hand.

Young slammed two cutting blows into Murphy, both just above the belt, driving wind out, but again Murphy did not feel it. He was not there to fight but to kill—to take and kill. Young tried to fight, tried to hit Murphy, but it did nothing. Three more times he struck out and Murphy took the blows without feeling them.

Murphy closed in, his left arm hanging uselessly at his side, closed inside of Young's blows and let the big man hammer on him, taking blow after blow. Then he reached with his right hand into Young's throat. Reached and closed and held, took all that Young could give him and held and squeezed, squeezed until the blows became feeble and he could hear Young's breath hissing. Squeezed until Young's arms flopped helplessly, squeezed until Young was on his back on the ground, Murphy holding him down. Squeezed until what had been Young was done, gone and done.

Then Murphy crawled away from the body to the

door of the shack, pulled himself up and staggered to the bunk and Midge. He was pulling air and sobbing and he told her that it would be all right, all right, all right. He touched the hair on her temple, touched it there and pushed it away from her eyes and knew that it would be . . .

Knew that it would be all right.

EPILOGUE

THEY WERE PACKING.

Nothing much because they didn't have much except each other. Murphy had thirty-two dollars and owed most of that to Doc for the medical work, except that Doc Hensley had refused to accept payment. Murphy had quit the town and they had nothing for him, not so much as a watch for the time he'd been there. Nothing but complaints because he was leaving right when they had a strike and the town would boom. Tonsun had taken the mine, legally staked a claim on it and retained Harris to run it for her. To be sure, it was the only true strike—called Wangsu's Honor—but optimism ran high that if there was one strike, there might be others.

Murphy had found an old freight wagon for five dollars, put new grease in the hubs, and they were packing. Wayne had sold him a teammate to go with the bay, a fifteen-year-old work mule that had some-how made it through the McCormick hole alive, and between the two horses they could pull the wagon. Slowly. But then Murphy and Midge weren't in a hurry to get anywhere, only in a hurry to leave.

From his office Murphy took only his own gear—one rifle, one shotgun, the Smith, and the clothes on his back. The rest, including the badge, he left when he walked out the door without looking back. After Doc fixed his arm, Murphy had spent six days taking care of Midge in the back of the café, talking in low tones to her, apologizing to her, being with her, and at the end of that time he had fixed the wagon, working one-handed, and they began packing.

It was morning and they thought to leave before noon. They would ride north and he would find work in Montana, work with his hands and back. Midge had saved eighty-five dollars to go with his thirty-two; they had flour and coffee and a slab of bacon and that was all Murphy wanted. That and to be shed of Cincherville.

Midge was bringing things to the door and handing them to Murphy, all without speaking, only the thing in their eyes between them. The wagon was nearly full when Murphy turned and saw Wong Ny standing there.

She was in the same blue tunic and pants, which caught the sun and made the colors come alive. She was carrying a small package in both hands. She stopped in front of Murphy, and Midge came to the door of the café. Wong Ny looked at both of them silently, her large eyes taking in them both, studying them in deep silence, then she handed the package to Midge.

"What . . . ?" Midge asked.

But Wong Ny turned and trotted off down the street, still silent.

Midge held the package and looked at Murphy. "What's this all about?"

"I think I know," Murphy sighed, watching the little figure trotting down the street. "I told her no—still, we're leaving and we could use it."

"Use what?"

"Open it."

Midge smiled uncertainly and pulled at the string holding the paper to the package. Then she tore the paper away. Inside, shining in the sun, cradled in her hands, lay a small, five-pound ingot of gold.

Traveling gold, Montana ranch gold, happiness gold, love gold, living gold, food gold—all that they needed lay nestled in her hands.

Murphy's gold.

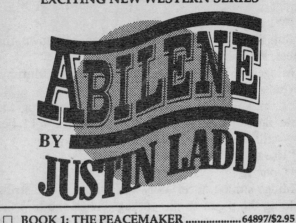